DATE DUE


```
Fic      Gideon, Melanie
Gid      The map that breathed
```

26299

The Map That Breathed

Stag's Head

Window
Woods

Lolan

Karain

Parth

Eila

Rivervillage

The Aggisto

Port City

Talfassa

The Map That Breathed

Melanie Gideon

Henry Holt and Company

New York

Abiding thanks to Benjamin Rewis, Sally Brady, and Reka Simonsen

Henry Holt and Company, LLC
Publishers since 1866
115 West 18th Street, New York, New York 10011
www.henryholt.com

Henry Holt is a registered trademark of Henry Holt and Company, LLC
Copyright © 2003 by Melanie Gideon
All rights reserved.
Distributed in Canada by H. B. Fenn and Company Ltd.

Library of Congress Cataloging-in-Publication Data
Gideon, Melanie.
The map that breathed / Melanie Gideon.
p.   cm.
Summary: When twelve-year-old Nora Sweetkale disappears into another world
through a "door" created by Billy Nolan, these two young people with extraordinary
abilities are caught up in a struggle with a powerful evil creature known as the Provisioner.
[1. Fantasy] I. Title.
PZ7.G3587Map 2003   [Fic]—dc21   2002038891

ISBN 0-8050-7142-3 / First Edition—2003 / Book designed by Donna Mark
Printed in the United States of America on acid-free paper. ∞

1   3   5   7   9   10   8   6   4   2

For Benji—future Traveler,
and for Dawn, Rebecca, and Sara—at whose side
I first stumbled upon the doorways
in South County

The Map That Breathed

Prologue

Police Chief Anil Avatar had forgotten all about the strange blue book with the imprint of the anchor on its cover. It had been sitting in a box in the basement of the police barracks for a dozen years. It wasn't until the afternoon of his last day of work that the book made its appearance, placed with reverence on his desk by a fawning young officer whose name Avatar could not remember.

"Lieutenant says this is yours, sir." The officer bobbed apologetically. "He says you'll know what to do with it."

Chief Avatar could not prevent himself from shuddering at the sight of the book. It brought back all sorts of unpleasant memories of a case he'd tried hard to forget. He'd never been able to make sense of it, which disturbed him, for he was a man who thrived on order and predictability. But what distressed him most was that he had been unable to set things right. Chief Avatar believed in helping people—it was why he had become a cop—but that night he hadn't been able to help anyone.

The young officer studied Chief Avatar closely for signs of physical weakness, but found none. The graying, slight man with tea-colored skin appeared as fit as ever. The officer loved and respected the chief, as did every man and woman who worked in the Waitsfield police station.

"Are you okay, sir?" he asked, having heard the rumors (which were false) that Avatar was retiring because of a weak heart. He was retiring simply because he was tired, having done the same thing for thirty-eight years.

The officer's concern made him uncomfortable. Avatar waved him away. "I need Bubble Wrap," he said. "Some string and some brown paper."

He knew exactly what he must do with the book. He had not lost track of Nora Sweetkale; Rhode Island was a small state and Waitsfield an even smaller town. Return property to rightful owner, he thought, suffering a moment of shame at the police department's oversight. He stared at the book, and his stomach contracted in fear. DON'T TOUCH, it seemed to warn him. Don't worry, he thought. He had no intention of doing so.

Chief Avatar sighed deeply. Only three more hours until he retired. Or so he wanted to believe.

Part One

Chapter One

Nora Sweetkale had always been a well-behaved girl. She made her bed every morning. She was pleasant to grown-ups. She rarely lied, and if she did, it was in order to spare somebody's feelings. She brought home As and Bs on her report card, and she was comfortably smart, which meant she had to study for her tests, but not too hard. She'd never caused her mother much worry. But all that changed when she got the blue book in the mail.

"Something's come for you," her mother said one afternoon, handing Nora a small brown parcel. Nora gave a little shriek of delight; she never got packages.

"There's no return address," her mother remarked. "Were you expecting something?"

Nora turned the package over in her hands and shook her head.

Her mother sighed, concern furrowing her brow. Pauline Sweetkale worked for Social Services; it was her job to be suspicious. "Well, you'd better open it and see what it is."

Nora nodded. She turned to leave the kitchen.

"Open it here," said her mother.

Nora bit her lip. For some reason she wanted privacy; she wasn't sure why. She sat down at the table and slowly unwrapped the parcel. She had the strangest sense that she was unwrapping something terribly important, something that would change her life. She unwound the Bubble Wrap carefully and gasped, for nestled in the plastic was a bird, its feathers turquoise and aquamarine, wings folded up tight against its body. And it was alive! She could see its breast heaving, its tiny heart pounding; it was panting for air. Nora clapped her hand to her mouth at the wonder of it. She looked up to gauge her mother's reaction, but her mother was digging around in the fridge, intent upon finding something; Nora had her privacy after all.

The bird's not from here, Nora thought. *It's not from this world.* She had never entertained such an idea before. Up until that moment she had been a practical girl who believed only in what she could see. But this bird . . . it seemed to suggest other possibilities.

The bird searched Nora's face with a surprisingly human awareness, its eyes glittering, full of grief. Nora wanted to comfort it. She reached out to touch it, but this was the wrong thing to do, for as soon as she placed her finger on its tiny head, the bird vanished and in its place was a book, its cover and pages the exact hues of the bird's feathers.

"So what is it?" her mother asked, turning around, a package of celery in her hands. She swooped over to pick the book up.

"No!" Nora shouted and clutched the book to her chest.

"Why, Nora! Whatever's wrong with you?"

"It's mine, it was sent to me. I should be allowed to look at it first," the girl protested. She felt as if she would burst into tears.

Her mother looked at her, eyebrows raised in surprise. Her mouth opened as if to say something, then closed as she decided that the book was harmless and she needn't be worried.

"You're right. It is yours. Off with you, then." Her mother started making the salad for supper.

*　　*　　*

Nora went up to her bedroom. The book stayed a book, but its animal presence remained, and instinctively she knew she must hold it close to her body.

She gently opened it, crooning to it softly. When she ruffled through the pages (which were empty, it was a blank book) there was the unmistakable sound of wings beating in the air, and Nora knew she hadn't imagined what she'd seen. The book was alive, if barely so, and it needed her to survive.

The first days with the book were wonderful. It was as if Nora had a newborn baby, dependent on her for everything. It was lovely to feel so wanted and needed. She took the book every-where. She pressed it close to her chest, believing this was the right thing to do. But as the weeks passed, its dependence on her gradually developed into something darker, more insistent, and Nora's moods grew darker as well, until one day she knew the truth: She was a prisoner of the book.

*　　*　　*

It was suppertime. Nora glanced at the book, which she had placed on the dining-room table. She knew all too well the consequences for letting it out of her sight. Agony.

At first she had only experienced a small tug when she forgot it or left it behind, a kind of breathlessness that was merely uncomfortable. But that tug very quickly turned into something much bigger, an acute pain, as though inside her body her bones were being shattered and the splinters were erupting through her skin. Despite the pain, Nora still felt liberated at the sight of the book. She hadn't forgotten the wonder and mystery of it; how it had first appeared to her as a bird, its true form. She believed the book was connected to her future and if she could just bear the pain, if she could just be awfully brave, she would realize her destiny. The book was merely testing her allegiance.

Nora set the table loudly, slamming the silverware down. She was surprised by her dreadful behavior but even more horrified at her inability to control her temper; it descended upon her like some wild animal, pinning her down at whim. This had been another side effect of assuming responsibility for the book, a less painful but more troublesome one. Sometimes she felt like her old lighthearted girl-self, wanting nothing more than to do errands with her mother and play I Spy with her three-year-old brother, David. Other times she felt so grim and heavy, so unlike her family, that she couldn't breathe.

Ms. Sweetkale took the fish sticks out of the oven and sighed. The familiar look of distaste was on Nora's face, the one that signaled the start of her violent moods. Puberty had hit Nora like a sudden storm, and her mother was trying to get used to the changes. She missed her old daughter, the one who confided in her, who had never had a sullen moment in her life. Nora had always wondered about the unfairness of losing both her mother and father in an airplane crash shortly after she was born, but now she was beginning to question her adoptive mother's shortcomings.

"Not again, Nora," her mother warned, having no intentions of being held prisoner by her daughter's moods.

Nora didn't answer. She poured herself a glass of milk and stared, her gaze a direct challenge.

"You want to go to Moonstone Beach, we'll go to Moonstone Beach," her mother relented, finally succumbing to Nora's request that she be taken there tomorrow. It was thirty miles from Sand Hill Cove, the beach they usually frequented. She slid a pat of butter onto the broccoli. "I just hope the waves aren't too much for David. It'll be no fun for him if they are."

Nora said nothing. Her mother looked up. "And Nora, we are not going to have the father conversation again, so don't even think about starting it."

"Why not?"

"Because it's ridiculous. You do not just ask for a father."

"But couldn't you just work on it a little? You could dress up a bit more, wear a little makeup, act a little interested," said Nora meanly, shocked at what was coming out of her mouth.

She couldn't believe she was saying this stuff out loud. It was, however, the truth. Nora had become embarrassed about her mother. Her mother was fifty-two, older than all of Nora's friends' mothers. She was dowdy. A bit overweight. She had stopped wearing lipstick years ago. But what Nora had become most dissatisfied with was being in a single-parent family. She wanted a father. She wanted their family to be four, not three.

"Young lady!" shouted her mother. "You are out of line. I'm going to tell you this just once more, and that's the end of it, *forever*. You, David, and I are a family. You don't need a father to complete *you* or to make *us* a family. You and I became a family the day I adopted you, and David became a member of our family the day we adopted him. You can't sit around waiting for a father to appear. Maybe someday you will get a father. Maybe you won't. And maybe you'll have to choose one yourself. Now, get your brother and let's eat. I don't want to hear another word about this."

*   *   *

That night after dinner Nora decided to go straight to bed.

"Should I be worried about you?" Her mother stood at the bottom of the stairs, a dish towel in her hands. "Is there something you want to tell me?" she asked softly. She had not given up hope that Nora would confide in her.

David ran by with a roll of paper towels.

"I'm fine, Mom, I'm just tired," Nora said, feeling horrible about the way she had been acting. "And I'm sorry. I won't ask about a father anymore." She looked down at her hands. "I know I've been kind of a jerk."

Her mother studied her for a moment. "I know you're sorry. Go take a bath. You've had a long day."

Nora nodded wearily. Her mother's kindness made her want to cry. She had never felt farther away from her, yet she felt incapable of closing the distance she had put between them.

After her bath Nora climbed into bed and held the book in her hands. She leafed through it. Not a word, not a sentence was written upon the pages; still it felt heavy and full of import. The book was very old, its paper wrinkly and parchmentlike, and it had a strange sort of anchor embossed on the cover. The binding was blue leather, discolored in many places where the oils from somebody's fingers had left their mark. Nora felt as if she and the book were feeding each other, bringing each other to life. This was her secret, but it was also her burden. She shut off the light and closed her eyes.

*　　*　　*

At eight o'clock on Saturday morning, Moonstone Beach was deserted. The early morning fog slowly dissipated, leaving behind a weak sun and patches of watery blue sky. It was late May in Waitsfield, but it was still cool in the mornings. Nora sat on a beach chair bundled up in a sweatshirt. Her mother and David were wandering up and down the shore, searching for sand dollars; it was too cold to swim.

Nora glanced down at the blue book, which lay open on her lap. Her throat swelled with emotion. She felt completely alone. Oh, how she wished she were young again, when life was made good by something as simple as an afternoon on the beach with her mother, the promise of ice cream, a beloved television show after a warm bath. Nora looked up from the book, its blank pages still eluding her, and saw a boy and a woman. They hadn't been there a minute ago; the fog must have shrouded them. They seemed to have just popped into the world.

Nora stared. In the burnished light the sight of them was jolting; their hair was the color of beets. The woman's hair hung down to her waist. Nora could see only the top of the boy's head, for he was sitting in a hole in the sand.

She tucked the book into her knapsack, slung it over her shoulder, and walked toward their blankets. She gazed back and forth from the Fluffernutter sandwiches the woman was unpacking to the boy. He had dug such a large hole that all Nora could see of him were his eyes and a slice of his crimson head.

The woman held out half a sandwich. A turquoise scarf kept her thick, curly hair back from her face. Her face was freckled, her green eyes bright; she was beautiful. Nora found herself tongue-tied. She imagined what it would be like to have such a glamorous mother.

"I'm Meg," the woman said. "And this is Billy." She pointed down into the hole in the sand. "Hungry?" she asked.

Nora said no, shyly.

"Well, then, how old are you?"

"Twelve," Nora said, shifting her weight nervously from one foot to the other.

"You've got a shining brow," Meg said softly, reaching forward to push the hair from Nora's forehead. "Know what that means?"

Nora shook her head.

"It means you're special. Meant for great things, but you know that, don't you? That's not news to you, eh?" She had a strange sort of accent.

For a moment Nora was not sure if Meg had even spoken, or if she had just wished the woman would say these things to her and so imagined it. Meg continued to smile at her, and Nora knew she had heard correctly. She was flooded with confidence and hunger. She wanted more of this, of somebody listening to her so intently, awaiting her next words. She wanted to bask in this woman's presence.

Meg Nolan had that effect on nearly everyone she came into contact with, so Nora's response to her was not unusual. What *was* unusual was her response to Nora, although she wouldn't speak of that to Nora, not yet.

Meg and her husband, Satchel, grew the tastiest, most succulent produce in all of Waitsfield. Their farm stand on Curtis Corner Road was very popular. All the children who frequented Nolan Farms with their parents fell under Meg's spell. She slipped them licorice whips, homemade potato chips, cups of apple cider.

The mothers of these besotted children did not always share the same sentiments about Meg, which was not surprising. They were envious. There were actually some people in Waitsfield who wished ill on Meg Nolan and her family, and this was not surprising either. It was often this way with people who were deemed too lucky or too content, people who appeared to have more than their fair share of happiness or bumper crops.

"Go on now, he's waiting for you," Meg said.

"Who's waiting?"

"Billy."

Nora looked startled. "But how did he know I'd be here?"

"He didn't. He's waiting all the same," said Meg.

Nora walked toward the hole. "Hey," she called down.

"Hey," Billy said back.

Nora looked at Meg as if for permission to continue.

"Go ahead. There's nothing to be afraid of. Billy's a bit shier than most. He keeps to himself. He's eleven, so you're older than he is. Don't forget that. You must be gentle. You must guide him," said Meg. "Or maybe he'll guide you." She laughed.

Meg spoke to Nora as if she were an adult. As if she was embarking upon a great journey. As if everything was fraught with significance. This was the way Nora wanted to live. She climbed into the hole with Billy.

"Or perhaps you'll guide each other," Meg Nolan whispered to herself.

Billy nodded at Nora solemnly and moved over to make room for her. His eyes were pale green, lighter than his mother's, the color of the inside of a lime. He did not look like he needed Nora to be gentle with him. He looked as though he could take care of himself perfectly well, and this was true, up to a point. Billy Nolan was very smart and used his intellect in place of the muscles he lacked, for he was a small, skinny boy, often beat up and always the last to be chosen for a team (unless it was the math team). He scrutinized Nora, looking deeply into her eyes, appeared to make some sort of internal decision, and turned away to face the wall of sand.

"Do we know each other?" Nora asked. She felt confused.

"Nope," Billy said.

Nora's heart fluttered as she sat alongside Billy. Being next to him electrified her. She had no idea why. Perhaps because he was Meg's son. She stole looks at him and saw he was nervous too. His bangs were damp with sweat.

Billy barely looked like his mother at all except for the color of his hair. He was puny, much shorter than Nora, all knees and elbows and pale skin—bluish, like skim milk. He had dark circles under his eyes, and Nora could see he bit his nails. Still, there was something about him she immediately admired, a stillness, an inherent trustworthiness. This was not a boy who would blab.

"What are you doing?" Nora asked.

"I'm making a window," said Billy, smoothing the sand in front of him with the palms of his hands.

"What's a window?"

"This."

Billy pulled his hands back, and the sand changed from a toast color to a pale blue, and then suddenly it became transparent and they were looking into a cavern of a room that was empty except for a long table and ten high-backed chairs. Nora stared at Billy in disbelief.

"Has this happened to you before?" she whispered.

"Yes," he said, a hint of impatience in his voice.

"What is this?" she asked.

"*Where* is this?" Billy corrected her. "Greenwater. The archipelago of Sanasarea. My best guess is that it's a meeting room of sorts, but I don't know for sure."

"And where's Sanasarea?" asked Nora, getting a funny feeling in her stomach, hoping he'd say someplace like Antarctica but knowing he wouldn't. The scene they were looking at struck her as beyond foreign—it was of a different time, a different place, like her blue book.

Billy looked at her with disappointment, his large eyes unblinking.

"You must take more chances," he said. "You must learn to trust your instincts. Yes, it's another world." He sighed, as if she were a child who had asked him the same question over and over again.

Billy had always found it easy to feel compassion for people. He would imagine being this person or that and so have a good idea of what they were thinking and feeling. Recently this sensitivity had intensified, and occasionally Billy was able to hear what people were thinking. With Nora it was as though he were listening to one side of a phone conversation. He had to make a conscious effort to stop eavesdropping; otherwise her thoughts assaulted him. Before she had even come over to their blanket, he had known about her sadness, about the strange book she carried in her knapsack. He was well aware that she was trafficking with the unknown, the unexplainable, like he was. That was how he knew he could trust her.

Nora bristled at Billy's impatience and was about to tell him she didn't appreciate being treated like a dummy when he said, "Look, over the fireplace, it's a painting." The window blurred and refocused like a camera lens, zooming in on the painting.

"It hears us," she said, clutching Billy's arm in fear. "It thinks we want to see the painting."

"You need to be careful what you say around windows," he said, gently detaching her hand from his arm. He was not used to being touched by kids his own age. Nora was so flabbergasted about looking into another world that she didn't even notice Billy pulling away from her. He was glad of this; he didn't want to offend her. He knew he sometimes came off as rude, but really it was a matter of inexperience. He had never slung his arm around a buddy, never entwined legs with somebody on the monkey bars.

The large rectangular painting was nearly three feet across. Four egg-sized emeralds were embedded in its gold frame. Billy and Nora were filled with a sense of foreboding. It was like the feeling you got right before the teacher handed back a math test, or in the seconds before a softball descended and everyone cleared, giving the signal that it was your catch.

"It's a map, not a painting," said Billy as they got closer.

The map was of an island called Talfassa. Four ribbons of color wound through the deep green countryside. They were labeled Lolan, Karain, Parth, and Eild.

"Are they rivers?" asked Nora.

Billy shrugged. "Beats me."

Closest to the Greenwater Sea was Port City, and in its central square was a large marble building labeled "The Aquisto." There were manicured lawns and lush gardens, terraces and wide sandy beaches. Up in the hills was a forest called Window Woods, and the highest point of the island was labeled "Stag's Head."

Suddenly the map darkened as if someone had dimmed the light. Billy and Nora looked up at the sky. There were no clouds; the sky was a brilliant blue.

"Did you see that?" whispered Billy.

A fetid wind came barreling out of the window, and sand whipped around in the hole. The two of them watched in astonishment as the map trembled and inhaled.

"It's breathing," gasped Nora. "The map is breathing!"

"More like struggling to breathe," Billy said, and it was true. The map seemed to fight for each ragged shallow breath.

"Ugh, what *is* that?" Nora grimaced and pinched her nostrils shut. "Tell me that's seaweed or rotten fish."

In the next instant the elaborate and breathtaking map of Talfassa was entirely blotted out, and another image began to surface, swimming toward them at great speed. Although the children were filled with dread, they did not climb out of the hole.

"Don't," Nora cautioned Billy, sensing he was about to shriek, as a face of colossal proportions bobbed up to the surface of the map. It looked normal in that it had two eyes, a nose, and a mouth, but the resemblance to anything human stopped there. Its skin was stretched taut across its face, straining against the bones. Its flesh, if you could call it that, was an unearthly hue, a dull pewter. Its features had the sly look of a giant fox. When it saw the children, its lips peeled back from its teeth in a frenzy. It looked at them hungrily, as if it would gobble them up. Nora peered into its cavernous mouth and saw something spinning around in there. A bird? A dragonfly? Something winged and frantic, struggling for life.

"It's swallowed something!" cried Nora. She had forgotten her own warning to Billy to remain quiet.

Long yellowed fingernails crusted with dried blood gripped the edges of the gold frame as the creature attempted to pull itself out of the map and into the hole the children were sitting in.

"Billy, time for lunch!"

At the sound of Meg's voice the thing slowly sank back into the depths of the map, which froze, as if deeply distressed, and then went perfectly still. The window disappeared.

Billy put his finger to his lips. "Not a word," he whispered, and they climbed out of the hole.

By that time it was nearly two in the afternoon. Nora's mother and brother had joined Meg almost an hour ago and they had been chatting amiably. Tomato-and-mayonnaise sandwiches were distributed. The bread was a bit soggy, but still it was a huge relief to be out of the hole and sitting on the blanket all together in the sun-light, eating lunch when lunch should have been all but over.

"Imagine that," said Meg, admiring Billy and Nora sitting side by side, "you living not even a mile away."

"Do you think it would be safe to let them bike on Curtis Corner Road?" asked Nora's mother.

Neither Billy nor Nora said more than a few words to each other for the rest of that afternoon. They were exhausted and bewildered. Their arms and legs felt noodly and weak, as though they had just gotten over the flu. They let their mothers arrange to have them meet on Monday, after school.

Chapter Two

It was a beautiful day in the archipelago of Sanasarea. The shores of each of the 109 islands were awash in brilliant shades of pink and red; the sea roses had just bloomed.

Molly Berry stood on the rocky shore of Berry Island, her spyglass up to her eye. Her little brother Roane stood beside her. They were looking for the Mapmaker, Asa Trout.

"See anything, Mol?"

Molly didn't answer. This was not unusual. She was often preoccupied, deep in thought. Roane was used to this. He never took it personally. Molly peered through her spyglass at the dense forest. A flash of red streaked by.

"Tria," she whispered sadly, letting the glass fall. It hung on a piece of rope around her neck. "Things are not well," she muttered. "One of these days I'm going to row across to see for myself."

Roane nodded at Molly, and she had a momentary flare of affection for her seven-year-old brother. He *was* loyal, she had to give him that. She had said the same thing many times, but she had never rowed across and probably never would. It was not her way. She avoided contact with other people whenever possible.

Molly was a Rememberer, so her job was to research, discover, absorb, and relay information. She had long black hair, and her blue eyes were vivid. She had the typical pale skin of her kind; Rememberers spent most of their time in the library memorizing texts. Roane was the opposite. He was a Grower. He spent all of his time in the gardens and fields. His cheeks were ruddy, his nails never clean. He knew all the cycles of the moon.

Even from across the water, Molly and Roane could see that Trout Island was in trouble. Debris littered the beach: driftwood, an old barrel, clumps of seaweed. A sour smell floated across when the wind was southerly—as though something had died or, at the very least, was rotting slowly.

Only once had they caught a glimpse of Asa Trout. It must have been almost three months earlier. He had been picking his way carefully through the trees just before sunrise. It was shocking. He looked horribly unwell, as if something was devouring him from the inside out. Something was terribly wrong.

Molly, like everyone else in Sanasarea, had often wondered about Asa Trout, who, after making the Map twelve years ago, had all but disappeared from Sanasarean society. Had Asa been merely bedraggled when Molly caught sight of him, she wouldn't have taken any special interest. She may have felt pity, enough to send Roane across the channel with a bit of food and a jug of wine, but nothing more; Molly was not known for her compassion. But a failing Asa Trout was something of a different order, and Molly had been deeply startled and disturbed at the sight of him. The very next day, Molly had begun conducting a stakeout with the hope that she had found the subject matter for her first Lifework: Asa Trout and the Map That Breathed.

Molly had just turned eighteen and at the end of the summer would graduate from the Remembery, nearly at the top of her class. Unlike the rest of her classmates, she still hadn't declared a topic for her Lifework, a treatise advancing an original point of view. The first Lifework was a good indicator of a Rememberer's future. If it was a mediocre blueprint, structurally weak, not sound of beam and foundation, the Rememberer's future would be mediocre as well. If it was luminous, a cathedral of visionary thinking, then the Rememberer's career would be brilliant. Everything hinged upon the first Lifework. Before she saw Asa Trout, Molly had told herself she hadn't found a topic because she was far more discriminating than her peers, but secretly she had been worried. Perhaps she didn't have what it took to be a first-rate Rememberer, and this was what she wanted to be, on the order of Dallan, the oldest and most esteemed Rememberer alive. After she saw Asa, Molly knew her waiting had not been for nothing. She was on the trail of something big.

She would need to present some proof, some evidence that would convince Dallan to give her access to the Deeps, where the shelves were filled with the most arcane and mysterious artifacts and books: items of the utmost power from different worlds, which Molly believed held the answers to her questions about Asa and the Map.

"Is it true? Did Asa really trap the Provisioner in the Map? And did the Map really breathe? Did you ever see it breathe?"

asked Roane, tugging on her skirt, pulling her abruptly from her thoughts.

Only for the first weeks after Asa had made the Map did it breathe. As the months passed, the Map seemed to lose its will for living, and eventually it became flat and one-dimensional, like a painting. Even though the Map no longer breathed, it was still revered because tangled somewhere in its depths was the Provisioner.

Molly sighed, resenting the interruption. Every summer she had to get used to communicating with people again. She found it hard going against her nature, even with her brother. She tried to make her smile warm.

"Yes, it's true. With my own eyes, I saw the Map breathing," said Molly. She had been very young; she hadn't even begun school yet. She remembered waiting in line for a long time and finally having her turn. It was one of the most memorable moments of her life—standing beside her father, gazing up at the Map. It was the first magical artifact she had ever seen, and it had lit a fire in her for more information, more knowledge.

"Tell me again about the Provisioner," the boy pleaded.

"Roane! Haven't you had enough of this by now? It's all you and your friends talk about at the Growery; don't think I don't know it."

"Tell me again anyway," said Roane. "You tell it so much better than me."

"Very well," said Molly, feigning annoyance. Actually she loved to pass on information. She was at her very best when given the opportunity to lecture.

"The Provisioner was a giant, over six and a half feet tall. It wore layers of furs no matter what the weather, furs that were soiled and matted with dirt. But the most unsettling thing was the Provisioner's face. It had features like yours or mine, but its skin was thick and hard. Its face looked like it was made from metal."

"But how did it steal the souls?" asked Roane. Like most children, he was hungry for the gory details.

"The Provisioner had a special bridle and bit just for that purpose. It approached from behind, and before the child even heard its footfalls, it slid the bridle over his head, buckled it tight, and placed the bit between the child's jaws, wrenching his mouth open. Once the bit was in place, the soul came streaming out."

Roane shuddered. "What did the soul look like?"

"Some say it was like a white smoke. Others say it was more like a ribbon, and still others swear it was like a river frothed up and milky from the spring melt."

"What happened to the soul once it came out of the child?"

"The Provisioner swallowed it, of course," said Molly, "for a soul is what was lacking. That's why it's called a Provisioner—it had to provide itself with a steady diet of souls in order to survive. The child was left an empty husk. For a few months the child held on but never longer than that, for what creature can live without a soul?"

"And there was no way to fight back? No way to kill the Provisioner?"

Molly shook her head. "None that we had ever discovered until the night Asa Trout made the Map."

"How do we know the Provisioner is *really* trapped inside of the Map?" asked Roane. Nobody had ever seen the Provisioner in there. They had all just taken Asa's word for it.

Exasperated, Molly frowned at her brother—she had told this story many times, and always Roane asked the same questions.

"We know the Provisioner is inside the Map because Asa told us so, and the Map is extraordinary for many reasons, the least of which is that Asa attended the Cookery," she said huffily.

"And it's extraordinary that someone from the Cookery would have the skill to make the Map?"

"Precisely."

"Well, suppose he didn't belong at the Cookery?"

"Are you saying Abundia left the wrong sign?" asked Molly. "Abundia never leaves the wrong sign."

"But a parent could understand it wrong," said Roane.

"Well, I suppose she could," Molly mused.

All the children in Sanasarea were visited by Abundia on the third evening after birth. Nobody ever saw Abundia coming and going, but what was left in the morning, surrounding the child's bassinet or nestled in the blankets, was a sign of his or her fate. Now the thing about Abundia was that, true to her name, she normally left an *abundant* sign of the baby's vocation that could not be mistaken. Pails of milk encircling a cradle signified a dairy farmer; a basket full of paints, an artist; a satchel of medicinal herbs, a healer. It was because of Abundia that parents knew exactly which of Sanasarea's twelve schools their children would be attending: the Healery, the Colory, the Growery, the Remembery, the Cookery, the Writery, the Acrobatery, the Beautery, the Gossipery, the Oraclery, the Musicery, or the Tomfoolery.

"Well, Asa's mother *was* a student at the Gossipery," said Molly. "And those Gossiperians have been known to stretch the truth. However, we cannot assume that she simply made up the crate of raisins that Abundia brought. That's unheard of! No parent would lie about her child's destiny sign."

They were both silent for a moment. "You never forget anybody's sign, do you, Mol?" said Roane.

"I've got a long and stellar memory," said Molly. One of the gifts, or curses, of being a Rememberer, she thought to herself. "Anyway, whether Asa belonged at the Cookery or not is neither here nor there, for he made the spectacular and *powerful* Map. Nobody can dispute that. A Map so powerful it imprisoned the Provisioner." Molly shook her head. "What I don't understand is what's happened to Asa. He disappeared after he made it, as if making the Map bled something out of him. And you saw him, Roane. He looks near death. How do we account for that?"

Roane shrugged, content to let his sister struggle with that puzzle. It was not his way to struggle with his mind, only with weeds.

Suddenly Molly realized she had all the evidence she was going to get to convince Dallan to let her into the Deeps. There simply wasn't any more. She hoped Asa's state would be enough to make her case. It would be an honor and a sign of great promise for a Rememberer to be let into the Deeps at such a young age. It was also a risk. One that she and Dallan would have to weigh carefully. If Dallan let her into the Deeps and she wasn't ready, the consequences could be fatal. Not only would the books and artifacts remain sealed to her, offering up none of their wisdom, but also they might seek to punish her for her audacity. It had been known to happen. Remembering was a dangerous profession.

"But we don't have to think about it because the Map has imprisoned the Provisioner for good," said Roane. "Right?"

He was worried, but Molly did not notice his need for re-assurance.

"Mmmm," said Molly distractedly. "Come on." She motioned to Roane to get the basket. "You get the kelp, I'll get the dulse. It's almost time to go to the market, and we'll not go empty-handed."

* * *

Life in Sanasarea had indeed been very good ever since Asa had trapped the Provisioner in the Map. The marsh grass grew tall and flourished, the storms were never really bad, the winters were not harsh, and from early April right through September, rasp-berries grew on the southern shore of every island, from Rote to Petucket. The crabs and lobsters were so plentiful you could sim-ply dip your hands in the water and catch them. The creels were full of fish every evening, and the orchards brimmed with peaches, apples, and pears.

There was always wood smoke in the air, sharp and tangy, mingling with the pleasant aroma of meat roasting and bread baking. Dogs were fat and happy, and jewel-colored doublecats bounded by at every corner, streaking through the trees.

All the seasons were celebrated in Sanasarea, and each had its own holidays and festivals, but summer was the best of all. In summer, the twelve schools let out, children went home to their family islands, and the public market opened every day, not just once a week.

The rules in Sanasarea changed during the summer. Work was allowed only between the hours of eleven and twelve in the morn-ings. Everyone slept late, woke up to drink strong coffee sweetened with honey, and lay down again in the shade for a mini-doze. *Then* they went to work. But laundry was not really work when everyone was flicking wet sheets at one another as they draped them on the limbs of trees to dry. Gathering blueberries for the evening's dessert was an event, as was digging for clams or cleaning mussels. It was much more fun when everyone got in on it. Work was only work when you had to do it alone.

After a leisurely lunch, everybody climbed in their boats to make the trip to Camarata, the main island of Sanasarea. The channel that ran in front of Camarata was called Eilon's Way, and it overflowed with bobbing vessels and brightly colored sails. Women leaned out of their boats and gossiped with one another. They passed bolts of fabric, clumps of grapes, and dog-eared books back and forth. Young men eyed young women, and then looked aloof after getting their attention. Children jumped into the water and floated up to other boats to be pulled aboard and given glasses of birchade and towels. Eventually everyone tied up and went to the public market to do the day's shopping.

There were stalls of beets and chard, radishes and asparagus, quail and partridge. There were also booths of toys—kites and chess games, dolls and whirligigs. There were service stalls: fortune-tellers, teeth-wrenchers, sock-finders, professional flea-removers. The most popular booth was for ear-pulling. There was always a long line at that one. Nothing like a proper ear-pulling to clear one's head, and everyone knew it wasn't something you could do yourself. It took a subtle tweak and a wriggle. Only under the fingers of an experienced ear-yanker could a difference be felt, otherwise it simply hurt.

After the day's marketing was done, a bell rang to announce the beginning of summer school. Everyone attended, not just the children. All the schools held special classes. There was "Pudding Sculpture" at the Cookery, "Holding Your Breath for Three Minutes" at the Acrobatery, "How to Get Someone Breathing Again" at the Healery, and "Admiring the Mule-Faced Skunk" at the Beautery.

After classes let out, pink umbrellas popped open like flowers on Camarata's beaches. A fierce badminton match was always going on, as well as croquet. Tipsy and overloaded, bicycles with giant wheels, five seats across, bustled down the dirt roads. And then, if there was not a special festival (though more often than not there was), families would drift home to barbecue their dinner. Little boys and girls caught boggleflies and stuck them in jars, the rainbow powder from the boggleflies' wings smeared on their fingers and faces. Often there would be music and singing. There was always sand between your toes. Shoes were rarely worn. Summer was a joyful time, and Sanasareans, thanks to Asa Trout, were a joyful people.

*　　*　　*

It was late that evening when the Berry family came home from Camarata. The moon was full, and stars were strung across the sky like silver seeds. Lou, Molly and Roane's father, had hung a lantern from the bow of the boat, and a warm pumpkin-colored light shone down upon the water. The boat rode low, heavy with the day's marketing: a new hoe, seven yards of red calico, and a round of ice rolled in sod.

Roane was asleep as their father rowed them home, singing softly under his breath, and Molly was thinking—obsessing really—because tomorrow she planned to go to Dallan and present her case. Just what *had* happened to Asa Trout, and why had the Map stopped breathing? Molly intended to find out.

Chapter Three

"*A* Gatemaker," groaned Meg. "Can you believe it?"

It was late Saturday evening, and Billy was asleep. Meg and Satchel Nolan sat on the steps of the porch. It was a warm night. A drenchy night, Billy would have called it, the air moist and heavy, fragrant with lilacs and newly mown grass.

"I just never thought. I mean, I suppose I always wondered. Would he be the same? Would he be a Traveler? But a Gatemaker! Oh, Satch, what are we going to do?" Meg cried.

"There's nothing to do," he said calmly. "It's a gift, Meg, not a curse. It's his destiny. We've just got to get out of the way."

"Easy for you to say," she grumbled.

They had lived with a secret for a long time. Meg was from Sanasarea. She and Satch had always known there was a possibility Billy would be a Traveler like Meg, a person who had the ability to travel through doorways to other worlds just as Meg had done fourteen years ago when she came to Waitsfield. It was not unusual for traveling to be passed down in the maternal line. Meg and Satch had wondered if and when Billy would inherit the traveling gene. But now they knew Billy was not a Traveler; he was a Gatemaker, the one who had the ability to *make* those windows and doorways between worlds. Meg had never heard of a Traveler giving birth to a Gatemaker, so she and Satchel were very surprised.

"Oh, she was remarkable," said Meg. "Full of life. Wait till you meet her." She was talking about Nora Sweetkale.

Despite her concern for Billy, Meg was filled with a sort of happy anticipation. She had known immediately that Nora was a Traveler, Billy's Traveler, for Travelers and Gatemakers were always paired; they were bound to each other. She had had to fight hard not to show her reaction on Moonstone Beach. It was like being punched in the stomach. It was instinctive, the recognition of a fellow Traveler, and it had brought back all sorts of memories. It had been years since Meg had traveled. She had no use for her gift here in Waitsfield. Where would she go? She had everything she wanted: Satch, Billy, the farm. Still, the memory of the heady exhilaration of passing between worlds had never left her.

"A girl Traveler," said Satch. He chuckled. "Our Billy's going to have to come out of his shell."

"Don't make fun of him," said Meg. "This is serious. Aren't you worried? He doesn't realize what he's up against."

She hated not knowing what the future would bring, especially when it concerned her son. Billy had no idea there would be limitations. He would want to go through a doorway of his own creation, and he wouldn't be able to. It was not his destiny to travel; it was Nora's. Gatemakers could only open the doorways; they could never pass through them.

"I know full well what he's up against," said Satch. "He'll need to temper his arrogance once he realizes the full extent of his power. Having Nora around will help. He'll realize he can't be a Gatemaker on his own. He can open all the windows and doorways he wants, but without somebody to go through them, they're not worth a thing. It'll be good for him to be paired. He's been a loner too long."

Meg sighed. It would not be an easy life for her child. It had not been easy for Meg's Gatemaker, Asa Trout. He had suffered mightily. She had no idea what had happened to him. They were estranged, which made Meg very sad. This lack of contact was the only way she knew he had not lived out his true calling, for if Asa had been gatemaking, she would have known. Being a Traveler and not being in touch with your Gatemaker was like having a limb ripped off. Meg had learned to live with her loss, but she had never healed.

Satch pulled Meg near to him, sensing that tears were close.

Meg began to sniffle. "He'll get hurt."

"That he will. But not because he's a Gatemaker. Because he's human," said Satch.

"And we can't do anything to stop it?" she asked.

"No."

Much as she would like to, Meg would not be able to keep Billy from his fate. And really, even though she was scared at the moment, she was not the kind of mother who would ever dream of doing so. She and Satchel were from different worlds, but they both believed that children should learn to work things out for themselves.

"So when are you going to tell him there's a name for what he is?" Satch asked softly.

"I have no idea how to do it," said Meg. "How do I tell my son I'm from a different world?"

Satch thought about this. "Do you think he's made a doorway yet?"

"Oh, no. It takes years to learn to make a doorway. Asa didn't make a doorway until he was twenty. They're kids. They're just fooling around with windows."

"Well, I guess there's no hurry then," said Satch. "We'll just watch and see and wait for the right moment."

Meg nodded, relieved, and laid her head on Satch's shoulder.

*   *   *

Monday turned out to be sunny and warm. Nora was nervous all day at school, practically sick to her stomach; she didn't even eat her Tater Tots at lunch. She felt sure Billy and his window into Sanasarea were somehow connected with the arrival of her book. If destiny could have a smell, she thought, it would be the smell of Moonstone Beach right before the fog cleared: the sand, the brisk May morning, the Chap Stick she had smeared on her lips. She even wondered if the book was somehow responsible for their meeting, if it had drawn them together. Why else had she insisted her mother take her to Moonstone Beach? They never went there; it wasn't a kids' beach.

Nora shivered with a mixture of excitement and dread. She had no idea what to expect. If she was sure of anything, it was that *something* had been set into motion, *something* had begun, and it would do no good to stand in its way; it was much too powerful a force. Her mother picked her up after school and dropped her off at Billy's, with a plate of brownies covered in aluminum foil.

"I'll pick her up at six," her mother yelled, waving at Meg, who had stuck her head out the window when the car pulled into the drive.

"Great, see you then. Come on in, Nora, the door's open." Meg pulled her head back inside.

Nora climbed the Nolans' porch stairs slowly, looking at her feet. All of a sudden this seemed like a very bad idea. She wanted to throw up. When she got to the top of the stairs, she looked through the screen door. She could see down a hallway into the kitchen where Billy and his mother were sitting at the table. Meg was pouring raspberry Kool-Aid into Dixie cups.

"Come on into the kitchen, lamb. Let's have something to eat," Meg called out.

Nora simply unbuckled at the sound of Billy's mother's voice (nobody had *ever* called her "lamb" before), and she opened the screen door and walked in. She arrived, brownies in hand, with a look of bewilderment on her face, as though she had taken a long journey in the twenty steps between the front door and the kitchen.

Billy surveyed Nora over the rim of his cup. Her skin was the exact color of the inside of a Heath Bar. Her hair was thick and black, and she wore it shoulder length, parted in the middle with two little hanks pinned flat to her scalp with green barrettes. Today she wore a flowered shirt and jeans with an apple patch on the back pocket. Billy drank noisily and deeply, draining the

Kool-Aid, and then smashed the cup on the table with his fist so that it was a flat circle. It made a popping sound. Little bits of wax fell on the floor.

"Billy, stop showing off," said Meg, throwing the wadded-up Kool-Aid envelope into the garbage. She sank it. "Two points," she said.

Nora handed her the plate, and Meg peeled off the aluminum foil. "Mmmm, brownies," she said, and popped a square into her mouth. "Tell your mom thanks, but she needn't have." She stood up. "Well, I'm off. I'll be home around five."

"You're not staying?" Nora asked.

"I'll be right across the street if you need me. You two stop by if you get bored; I'll give you licorice whips." In the next instant she was gone, leaving Billy and Nora alone in the kitchen.

Neither of them said anything for a while. They stared at each other across the table.

"She's only across the street; look, you can see her from the window."

They got up and went to the living room. Sure enough, they could see her standing behind the register of the farm stand, weighing potatoes. She looked up at that moment and waved. They waved back.

"Red Bliss," said Billy a bit sadly. "Thirty-five cents a pound."

They watched Meg for a while, not saying anything. They both felt a bit bereft without her, and Nora wondered if she should call her mother. She was feeling sick to her stomach again. But then Billy asked, "So, want a tour?" and Nora nodded quickly so she wouldn't have to speak. She was afraid her voice would crack.

"You want to take your knapsack off?" asked Billy. "You can hang it next to mine." He pointed to a set of hooks in the hallway.

"No, thanks," Nora said, trying to act nonchalant. She realized she'd have to come up with a less conspicuous way of carrying the book. A purse perhaps; that would provoke less attention. Nora was not a girly-girl and did not relish the thought of carrying a purse, but what other choice did she have? Could she get away with carrying a knapsack all the time?

Billy shrugged as if it didn't matter one way or the other to him. He had been testing her. He knew the blue book was in the knapsack and that she didn't want to be separated from it, ever. Why that was the case he didn't know, nor would he allow himself to know. He had been shielding himself from Nora's thoughts by putting up a kind of mental filter that didn't completely stop the onslaught but let through every other word. In this way the transmission became gobbledygook. Billy understood the sanctity of privacy. He did not want to intrude, although he was extremely curious about that blue book.

The Nolans' house was nothing like Nora's house. It was much bigger. There were sixteen rooms, some completely empty, some only partially furnished. Some rooms had nothing but a vase of flowers sitting in the middle of the floor, as if awaiting a guest. Nora smelled clover.

"Incense," Billy told her. "Meg uses it everywhere."

"You call your mother Meg?" asked Nora.

"Sure, that's her name."

Nora was amazed. This family was nothing like hers. She never knew people lived like this.

"I think I should tell you that I'm an orphan," she blurted out.

Billy looked startled. "How can you be an orphan? You have a mother."

"I'm adopted. My real parents died in an airplane crash a couple of weeks after I was born. I thought you should know."

"Oh," said Billy. He felt uncomfortable with this sudden disclosure. He wasn't sure how he should respond. "It doesn't matter."

"It matters to me," said Nora. "That you know, I mean."

He nodded, unsure of what to say.

"So can you make another one?" Nora asked.

"A window?" Billy said, grateful to change the subject.

"Uh-huh."

"Yes. I think I can make a door, too. That will allow us to go through into Sanasarea."

Billy hadn't intended to share this information with Nora; it just came out. He was surprised by how much he wanted to impress her. He cringed immediately after he had said it. He sounded like a braggart.

Nora's arms riddled with goose bumps. She felt the book move in her knapsack. She heard it rustling around. She heard the sound of tiny claws scratching. She fought to keep her face from registering her shock and prayed Billy would not notice.

"Why do you think that?" she whispered.

Billy looked up. "I don't know, I just do. What's more important is, do you believe me?"

"Yes," said Nora without hesitation. "And when do you think you might make that door?"

"Soon."

"Oh." Her throat ached and she felt light-headed.

They heard the sound of a truck pulling up, gravel crunching beneath the heavy wheels.

"Dad," said Billy.

"Do your parents . . . do your parents . . . ?" Nora felt tongue-tied, unable to ask her question.

"No," said Billy. He didn't have to read her mind to know what she was thinking. "They don't know I make windows. They think I'm a normal kid. You're the only one who knows."

Satchel Nolan strode into the kitchen, two heads of lettuce in his hands. He was a big man, almost always dressed in clay-colored Carhartt work pants and an old plaid wool jacket. The house and the farm had been in his family for more than a hundred years. He was a Waitsfield native, down-to-earth and of the earth, a man whose favorite pastime other than farming was listening to the music of Ella Fitzgerald. He could be trusted and depended upon and was capable of fixing nearly anything. He was deeply devoted to Billy and Meg.

"You must be Nora." Satch walked over to shake her hand, his eyes bright. He studied her for a moment, a half-smile on his face. "Meg's right about you," he said.

Nora blushed. She knew exactly what he was talking about—Meg telling her she was special, meant for great things.

"Right about what?" asked Billy.

"She thought we'd like each other," Nora said quickly, not wanting to share the compliment with Billy. Wanting to keep it all for herself. She felt a pang of guilt, and Satch looked surprised but said nothing.

"She thought we might be friends," Nora added.

"Oh," said Billy, perfectly aware that she was telling a half-truth. "We were just about to take a walk." He turned to his father. "I was going to show her around the farm."

"Good idea," said Satch, tossing the lettuce in the sink.

*   *   *

Billy's family owned one hundred acres of woods, fields, and meadows. Nora and Billy tromped through the fields in silence under an enormous bowl of blue sky, heading toward the woods.

"The trail starts there." Billy pointed. Nora could see an opening in the trees, but the foliage was so dense, she wouldn't have known there was a trail if Billy hadn't shown her where it was.

"Does it go anywhere?" she asked.

"To Lily Creek, eventually," he said. "But I don't think we have time to make it there today."

Once they entered the woods, it got dark. Patches of sunlight broke through onto the trail, dappling the ground.

"Billy?"

"What?"

"Are you going to make another window? Is that why you're taking me here?"

"Yes."

"I was hoping you'd say that," said Nora. "But why here? Is there something special about this spot?"

"I try to make the windows far away from the house so that my parents don't suspect anything. Besides, I've always been able to make one in this place. Some places it's easier than others. I can't quite control them yet."

They walked for another fifteen minutes into an even denser wood. Billy held back the low, sweeping branches of a pine tree so Nora could pass, and when they looked up next they were standing in front of a small body of water.

"It's called the Little Swamp," said Billy.

The trees that lined the bank of the Little Swamp were strange and oddly formed. The branches were thick, gnarled, and twisted, creating a kind of ceiling.

Billy kneeled down, and Nora knelt beside him. He brought his hands up and began to make a circle in the air. His face was grim; he was concentrating. The air solidified, then became translucent, then thickened and quivered like jelly. Billy groaned softly with his effort. He made a rapid gesture, as if pulling back a curtain, and a scene materialized. They saw a cottage. Smoke was coming out of the chimney. They heard a man's voice. "Here, Tria, Tria, Tria." An enormous creature strolled into view.

"A doublecat," said Billy, and as soon as he said it, Nora knew it was true, for that was precisely what this animal was, a huge house-cat the size of a small pony. But the most astounding thing was its color, for Tria was the ruby pink of strawberry punch, and she wore a sapphire-blue collar that set off her vibrant fur beautifully.

Tria stepped daintily around a tree when she heard the man calling her, her paws rising and falling in the air, prancing like a horse. She seemed ready to go inside as she approached the door of the cottage, but suddenly she turned, lifted her pink nose into the air, and hissed.

Nora jumped, and covered her mouth, as if the sound of her breathing had alerted Tria to her and Billy's presence. The double-cat began moving toward them.

"Tria, in here NOW!" the man roared.

Like crabs, Nora and Billy skittered back from the window as it dissolved. It was twilight. They headed for home in a hurry, Billy leading the way. They were starving. By the time they got to the edge of the woods, the first stars were coming out.

"Meg's gonna be mad." Billy shook his head. "I always lose track of time when I make windows."

They could see his house on the other side of the field. It was all lit up. Nora thought of her own home, of her mother and David. All of a sudden she felt very tired; she wanted to go home.

"The man's name is Asa Trout," said Billy.

"How do you know that?"

"I just do."

"But how?" pressed Nora.

Billy did not want to tell her he could read people's thoughts. He wasn't sure if he could trust her with all his secrets yet.

"I just do," he said again.

She nodded, deciding to let it go. "So why didn't we see the map?"

"I don't know. That time on the beach with you was the first time I'd seen it. To be honest, I'm glad we didn't see it," said Billy.

They didn't speak of the horrifying creature they had seen trapped in the map. Neither of them wanted to remember it.

"This was much nicer. That cottage was painted the color of lilacs. And that cat—have you ever seen such a thing?"

"Never," said Billy.

They ran out of the field and into the backyard. Through the sliding glass doors they could see Meg taking a pan out of the oven and Nora's mother and brother sitting at the table.

"Uh-oh," said Nora, knowing she was in for it.

They clumped up the steps onto the porch. Meg heard them, threw her potholders down, and barreled out the door.

"Lambs, lambs, where have you been?" Meg gathered them up in her arms. She smelled like onions and garlic and chocolate. There was a steaming hot pan of lasagna on the counter and an unfrosted cake on the kitchen table.

Nora peered over Meg's shoulder at her mother, feeling guilty for being late and for being in Meg's arms.

"I'm sorry," she called out to her mother. "We just lost track of time."

Her mother looked at her coolly. She had been waiting for forty-five minutes but she would not berate Nora in front of the Nolans. That was not her style.

"Stay for dinner," said Meg, trying to smooth things over.

"That's kind of you, but Nora's got homework and I must get this little one into the bath," said Pauline, hugging David. She stood, holding out Nora's jacket. "Shall we go?"

Nora wanted desperately to stay, but of course she couldn't say that. She followed her mother out the door.

Chapter Four

*T*he day Asa Trout stole the Map from Sanasarea Hall was the day he saw the boy and the girl spying on him through a window in the aspen grove. Being spied upon was disconcerting enough, but to see a fellow Gatemaker (and such a young one at that) was even more disturbing; Asa had had nothing to do with windows and doorways for many years. That part of his life was over.

But as startling as it had been for him, it was even more so for Tria, since she was a temperamental creature. Still, Asa could not have predicted how Tria would react. As soon as she saw the children, she made for them, head up in the air, two-foot-long tail twitching and high, hissing the entire while.

Of course the children had been terrified, and the window had dissolved, but Tria was irrevocably irritated. She refused to eat. She licked her paws and looked at Asa haughtily, as if punishing him for whatever was going on. Unable to deny the growing unease that had been with him for weeks but had been made worse by that morning's strange event, Asa set off for Sanasarea Hall.

The hall was empty, as usual. It was never used, except for the seasonal meetings of the Best Interest Council, which was more interested in who had died and who had been born than the business of Sanasarea. The building was open, however, as always. Sanasarea Hall was like a place of worship—its doors never closed.

Asa loved the solemnity of the old hall: the papery smell of charts and old texts, the tang of ink, the spiciness of pencil lead. He went directly into the meeting room, where the Map was mounted over the fireplace. He missed Tria's presence. She would not enter the building, and this seemed like a bad omen to Asa. She waited for him outside by the fountain on the plaza.

Asa was a big man, and it was a big Map. He didn't know what he was going to do before he did it. He strode across the room to the Map and lifted it off the wall. Framed, it must have weighed nearly twenty pounds. He laid it down on the table so that he could have a good look and within seconds he was knee-deep in memory.

In his early years, Asa Trout had lived a happy enough life. He was loved by his mother and father. He was not a brilliant student at the Cookery, but neither was he at the bottom of his class. He studied hard; cooking never came easy for him, but he was a quiet and patient boy, well suited to memorizing recipes and the long hours of waiting for bread to rise. All that changed one July morning, the morning he turned twelve and woke to find a series of doorways, one inside the other, ridged on the palms of his hands.

"Ma!" he yelled, and jumped out of bed, a tall dark-skinned

child, eyes the color of topaz, hair shorn close to his scalp. He held his palms up for her to inspect.

Asa was not the kind of boy who kept anything from his mother, and his mother was not the kind of woman who would stand for anything being kept from her. Lila Trout was a bullet-tongued gossip, queen of the sharp word.

"Mercysakes!" she cried. "You're a Gatemaker!"

She grabbed Asa's hands as if they were her property and desperately tried to rub off the sign with the bottom of her apron. It was no good. The Kapth, the Gatemaker icons, were embossed on his palms for good. Lila Trout sank to her knees.

"I had prayed this day would never come!" she sobbed.

Asa was horrified. So his mother *had* lied about his destiny sign! He had suspected that this was the case. Nobody else at the Cookery had to work as hard as he did. He knew that was not right. Apprentices should have a natural aptitude. He had always felt he was fighting against a current, but never had he dreamed he was a Gatemaker.

"You did something," his mother charged, rising quickly, her finger stabbing the air. "You asked for this! You made this happen!"

"I didn't," Asa said calmly, used to her melodramatics. "I didn't do anything." But he couldn't keep the excitement from his voice. He was special. He would learn how to make doorways between worlds!

His mother's face darkened.

"If you knew what was ahead, you'd wipe that smile off your face," she snapped. "Think." She tapped her temple. "There's no place for you to go. No place for you to get educated. What kind of a life is that? I'll tell you what kind of life. A half-life. You'll never live out your destiny. That's nothing to be happy about, you silly boy!"

She was right. There was no school for Gatemakers in Sanasarea. The only school for Gatemakers in all of Greenwater was on Talfassa, and he could no more go to Talfassa than spit spiders.

The cruel turn his life had taken suddenly dawned on him. Asa looked out the kitchen window at the Veil, the ring of fog and mist that encircled all of Sanasarea. It looked benevolent. The mist was a beautiful sort of violet color. Even from thirty miles away Asa could hear the rhythmic *whoosh*. It sounded as if the Veil was constantly collapsing and building itself back up. But the Veil was made up of no ordinary fog; it was fog of a mind-twisting, disorienting, life-sucking kind. Nobody had ever returned from trying to pass through the Veil. It was said those who attempted it died a horrible death, suffocating, the blood spilling out of their ears, pouring out of their mouths, seeping out from beneath their fingernails. It was said only those purest of heart (or without a heart, like the Provisioner) could get through the Veil alive. But perhaps a child could, thought Asa. Perhaps somebody not yet tainted, somebody who did everything that was asked of him, who tried his very best, who caused nobody any problems. *Somebody like him.*

"I know what you're thinking," his mother said, intruding upon his thoughts. "You're thinking that you're different. That you'll make it through the Veil to Talfassa. Well, you won't. You'll stay right here where you belong, and I don't want to hear another word about it."

Lila Trout took off her apron and hung it on a peg. "Now, let me see your hands," she said, all business. She was not comfortable in the realm of possibility and chance. She believed only in what she overheard.

Asa presented his palms.

"No, the other side. It's your skin tone I'm after. I'd call that mahogany, I would. I'll throw in a bit of pink. The palms should be five shades lighter."

Asa felt sick to his stomach. "What are you planning?" he asked.

"Why, to hide the Kapth, of course. I'm going to make a camouflage paste. How else did you think you'd go on?" his mother said. "It'll be a different life for you now. One of secrecy. It won't be too hard," she continued, softening a bit when she saw the look of dismay on Asa's face. She tilted up his chin. "Look at me, boy. You've been doing this all your life. Passing. The only difference is now you know it. My advice to you is to forget all about being a Gatemaker. You'll suffer far less."

Asa nodded, tears spilling from his eyes. He felt as if he were being asked to stop breathing. His childhood was over in one night's passing.

"Ah, Asa, you belong here. You belong in Sanasarea. Don't set your spirit adrift," his mother said gently, seeing the mixture of terror and sadness on her son's face.

Asa wanted to believe he belonged there. He was a dreamy sort, not a hero, not somebody who had ever searched out adventure. But the truth was, his connection to Sanasarea was already severed. It had been cut the moment the Kapth appeared on the palms of his hands. He was already adrift and would be for a long time.

*   *   *

The weeks passed and Asa did as his mother told him. He returned to the Cookery; he did not experiment or attempt to make a doorway; and he tried to ban all thoughts of his real destiny. He began making the camouflage paste himself, a mixture of clay, bark, and dandelion juice, and every morning that he smeared it on his palms, erasing the truth of himself, a bit of him withered away.

He did allow himself to wonder. Did he have a Traveler? Was it a boy or a girl? Were there others like him in Sanasarea, other Gatemakers and Travelers who were living in secrecy? But nobody ever stepped forward, and Asa came to believe he was the only one.

And so Asa did end up living exactly the sort of half-life his mother prophesied he might. By the time he was twenty, he was a ghost of the happy boy he had once been. He had done all the things expected of him. He asked nothing of anybody. He might as well have been invisible, and that was the way he liked it. He decided to become a teacher at the Cookery mostly because it required very little contact with other adults. Asa was already a recluse, and he found it was only the children who would let him be.

*   *   *

One evening, a few months into the school term, Asa lay in bed in the Cookery dormitory, miserable and freezing cold. It was his month for dorm duty, a job he hated. The bed was too small for his large frame, and the students farted, burped, and snored all night long as a result of their rich diets.

It was November, and Asa was smack in the middle of teaching seventh grade, the year of Pastries, Cakes, and Dough. Most Cookery apprentices loved seventh grade, since they ate nothing but desserts for months at a time, but Asa's students were failing horribly. They could get nothing right. Their pie dough was either too mushy or too crumbly. Their croissants looked like tubas and tasted like baking soda, and it was all because their teacher wasn't a cook at all but a Gatemaker. Asa had already been spoken to by the Headmaster, a kind woman who encouraged him to try harder, to put everything into his teaching. The truth was Asa was horribly depressed. He felt like he couldn't go on much longer with his charade.

Blue light streamed in through the dormers, and Asa pulled down his covers and groaned. It was quite a storm. He couldn't believe none of the children had woken up, even though they were such sound sleepers, all of them drinking their butterscotch milk obediently every night before bed. Asa got up, knowing there would be no sleep for him now, not with this storm. He dressed quickly, put on his coat and hat, and went out into the night.

He glanced furtively to the left and to the right as he hobbled down the icy streets of Camarata. The Provisioner was back again after a two-week respite. Just last night a four-year-old child had been taken from the Healery. Asa did not really fear for his own safety; the Provisioner had never taken a child older than seven. Still, he'd left his charges alone, something he should never have done. He wondered if he should return to the dorm. He was behaving selfishly in his search for a few moments of solitude. Ah, they'd be okay, he told himself, with the resignation of a person who was accustomed to living in a siege state.

The Provisioner had been preying on Sanasarean children for a long time, so long that there had been more than one; the first had come nearly twenty-five years ago, stealing Sanasarea's innocence along with the souls of its beloved children. Where it came from nobody knew; just that it was somewhere outside the Veil. The Provisioner was impervious to the effects of the Veil, for it was truly a creature without a heart. The people of Sanasarea never knew when to expect it. A few peaceful weeks would go by, sometimes a month, but inevitably the terror would return.

Sanasarean children had learned to live with the Provisioner much like children in a war zone learn to live with the threat of bombs. They didn't take unnecessary precautions. They didn't go out alone after dark, but they also became accustomed to the danger, believing the bad thing would happen to somebody else. The children imagined a sort of protective bubble around themselves. How else could they go on living with the daily threat of death?

Breathless, Asa ran up the steps of Sanasarea Hall. As soon as he shut the door he felt calm. The hall was a refuge for him, a place of comfort. It was almost always empty, a blessed relief to Asa, whose days were filled with the babbling high-pitched voices of children. He climbed the stairs wearily and soon found himself at the entrance of the tower. He pushed open the door and walked into the center of the room.

There was a current of heat pouring down his arms and into his hands. He cursed. The wretched Kapth; they did this occasionally and it made him feel sick. He needed to mix up some more paste. He had run out yesterday and had been walking around hiding his hands all day. At the moment the Kapth were blue-black, the color of an angry bruise. They throbbed on his hands.

The storm raged on. There was a continual barrage of noise, as though someone were battering Sanasarea Hall with a giant broom. There were no lights, no wall sconces, nor even a candle, but there was no need of them; every few minutes lightning illuminated the room.

A painting was propped up on an easel in the corner of the room. This was odd. Asa came to the tower often, and the painting had never been there before. He walked over to the easel and to his surprise found the canvas blank. The canvas was framed ornately, with huge jewels embedded in the gold frame, yet it was unmarked. Asa peered more closely. He drew back in surprise. This was no ordinary canvas. Although it was white, there was a translucence to it, and it shimmered like mica. Life streamed below the surface.

Asa groaned. He found himself filled with despair in the presence of such a miraculous artifact. Here was all this wonderful potential, and Asa, with his dead end of a life, could do nothing with it. He shuddered and leaned his forehead against the canvas.

"I am lost," he moaned softly, his fingers spreading wide against the white surface.

To his surprise he found the canvas soft and yielding. It felt like he was poking into somebody's stomach. Asa pulled his hands back in alarm and saw ten small indentations that now oozed with color. Glimmering silver-blue filled the hollows, then spilled out of them and began to spread down the length of the canvas like a tongue.

The tower filled with the unmistakable sounds of a river; gentle swishing, water moving over pebbles. Asa could smell the river, clean and sun-drenched, and he leaned forward and touched the canvas again. There was the same yielding. His finger left another indentation that pooled up with orange-red, the color of embers. This fiery liquid arranged itself into another river. Soon another vein of color leapt across the canvas, this one a golden-rose, and Asa suddenly knew what was coming alive under his fingers. The canvas flowed with Talfassa's legendary four rivers of metal: the Lolan, the Karain, the Parth, and the Eild.

"Talfassa," he gasped, seeing the world that had been denied him springing to life. He was filled with hope, the kind he had exiled a long, long time ago. This hope saturated him, and he lifted his hands up to his face. The Kapth were glowing a leafy green now, as if they had been set free.

Asa touched the canvas again and again until the entire thing was covered with brilliant swaths of color and Talfassa was spread out before him. There was Port City, devoted to scholarly pursuits. Rivervillage encircled Port City. All the Riverdwellers lived there, the master craftspeople and artisans who worked with the metal from the four rivers. On the outer edges of Rivervillage, the land flared out gracefully like a scallop shell, from east to west. Hamlets were folded and tucked into the shadows of the hills, and the whole mass of it, all of Talfassa, was moving and trembling beneath his fingers. It was *breathing*.

The last things to appear on the canvas were words labeling the buildings and the rivers, and it was then Asa understood he had made a Map. He began looking desperately for the Aquisto, the school for Gatemakers and Travelers. Words skittered across the surface of the canvas. He felt that everything would be made clear if he could just find the Aquisto. He stepped closer.

In his excitement he stumbled and fell forward. He threw his arms out to catch himself but amazingly there was no need to. The canvas did not come clattering off the easel to the floor; it simply absorbed him. He literally fell into it, his entire upper body disappearing into the Map.

Half of him was in the tower, the other half in Talfassa. His upper body was in the central square of Port City. The streets were paved with marble. He could smell jasmine and baking bread. Gatemakers and Travelers strolled past him, arguing, their long robes blowing up behind them with the sea breeze. None of them gave him a second glance. Asa was stunned. He pulled himself out of the Map with such force he fell backward five feet. There was a loud sucking noise, and he was in the tower room once more.

He was panting. He took deep breaths to calm himself. Did that really happen? He had to try it again. He got up and walked back to the Map slowly. He stood in front of the canvas. He held on to the edges of the frame forcefully and this time stuck only his head in.

"Hallo," a young Traveler called out as Asa's head materialized in front of him, causing him to stop in mid-stride. "Are you coming to the Aquisto?"

Asa nodded, not knowing what else to do. The Traveler looked at him calmly, as if he were quite used to the sight of disembodied heads appearing out of nowhere.

"I'm trying," said Asa.

"Is that a window you're in?" the Traveler asked.

"It's a Map," said Asa.

The Traveler nodded. He had heard of stranger things. "Well, come on then," he said. "Don't dillydally. Looks like you've wasted enough time already. You're much older than most of the students here. But I shouldn't think that will matter much. They're an accepting lot."

"But how do I get there?" asked Asa.

"Just pull the rest of your body through," said the Traveler. "Don't worry. You're allowed to travel when you come to the Aquisto. Don't you know that?"

As a rule Gatemakers were not allowed to travel to other worlds. Making a doorway was a formidable power, and power had to be parceled out carefully; everybody was given just a bit so that nobody ever had all of it. There was only one time when an exception could be made, when a Gatemaker was going to the Aquisto. Then and only then was a Gatemaker allowed to pass through a doorway of his or her own creation. But this exception hadn't applied to Asa because he lived in Greenwater. He couldn't make a doorway into a world he already lived in, so the only way for Asa to get to Talfassa was to go on foot, and that would have meant passing through the Veil. Now it appeared Asa was being offered the opportunity to live out his destiny in another way, to get to Talfassa through the Map. Could it be this easy? Could he just step through?

Then Asa made his fatal mistake: He hesitated. It was his nature to be too cautious, to think things over.

"I'll be right back," he said.

The Traveler nodded. "I'll wait for you."

Asa retracted his head back into the tower room, and found he was no longer alone.

There are times when the legend is far worse than the reality. Times when you find out the horror stories are just that, stories. This was not one of those times. The Provisioner stood not two feet from Asa; it had crept up the stairs while he had been making the Map.

If the Provisioner had been purely a monster, something unrecognizable, perhaps Asa would have been able to keep his wits about him. But this was not the case. The sight of the Provisioner was far worse than Asa had ever imagined, and it terrified him at a much deeper level. What was most frightening was not its physical appearance: the cold, deadened eyes; the heavy, reeking furs it was swaddled in; the child-sized bridle and bit that hung from one enormous hand. The truly horrifying thing was that Asa could tell the Provisioner had been a man once. Its humanity hung from it in shreds like its clothing. Asa could sense its tattered memories, and they assaulted him, a ghastly mishmash of cruelty and abuse. The Provisioner had been flayed of its life, and now its mission was to skin others of theirs.

Asa's hands rose as if to deflect a blow that he knew was coming. The Kapth were emitting a blue light; sparks flew from them. The room crackled and glowed.

The Provisioner stalked toward him in a predatory fashion. Asa was stricken with fear. *But I'm too old,* he tried to say, but no words came out and he realized it didn't matter. The Provisioner clearly intended to harm him. Then Asa remembered the Map. *I'll wait for you,* the Traveler had said. Asa could escape all this; escape and find his destiny. Talfassa was waiting for him. He glanced quickly at the Map. It was still breathing. The rivers were flowing. The chosen Gatemakers and Travelers walked through its streets. This was his chance. He leapt at the Map, arms and legs paddling.

"No!" he screamed as he and the Provisioner collided in midair, both of them hitting the floor with a huge thud. The easel fell. The Map plummeted to the ground, and Asa went flying backward once more. He groaned as his head hit the door. The Provisioner fell on the other side of the room. It tumbled violently as it hit the ground and rolled onto the Map. The Map collapsed like a huge sinkhole beneath the weight of its body, all the brilliant color pouring inward as the Provisioner was swallowed up. There was a long shuddering ribbon of sound as the Map recollected itself and flattened out, and then there was silence.

Asa staggered to his feet, blood pouring down his temple, and ran to the Map, which was making a gasping sort of sound. He didn't care if the Provisioner was in Talfassa, he was going too! Asa jumped onto the Map. Nothing happened. He was simply standing on top of it. Asa picked it up and put it back on the easel. Perhaps he had to dive into it. He threw himself forward and the Map fell to the ground. Asa sank to his knees. He pounded on the surface of the Map with his fists, weeping like a child. And although the Map was still breathing, convulsing and writhing beneath him, it would not let him in, and Asa knew why. The Provisioner had fallen in instead. His only chance to go to Talfassa was gone; the Provisioner had stolen it. He was so distraught he did not think of the one good thing that had happened: The Provisioner was no longer there.

"Well done."

A young woman with long red hair stepped out of the shadows.

"Where did you come from?" Asa gasped.

The woman ignored his question and walked briskly over to him. She grabbed his hands, turning them over quickly.

"Let go!" he yelled, and pulled his hands back, but not before she had seen the Kapth.

"You're a Gatemaker," she said.

"You were here the whole time?" he asked. "You were watching? And you didn't help me?" He was humiliated and frightened. She had seen him trying to escape, seen him crying.

She seemed not to hear him. "What took you so long to make a door?"

"I didn't know I was supposed to," snapped Asa, getting angry.

"You never experimented? You were never curious?" the young woman asked, amazed. "You have unbelievable power. You can make doorways between worlds. How could you not use that power?"

"I was never allowed to. There is no future for Gatemakers in Sanasarea. Nor for Travelers," Asa recited his mother's creed obediently.

The woman sighed. "That's where you're wrong. Look, over there. You've made a doorway."

She pointed to a place where the air had pleated together. The door hung there, propped open. Through it they could see a creek shimmering in the moonlight.

"I did that?" asked Asa, bewildered.

"You did. I saw you," said the young woman. "That crackling sound. You know, when you held your hands up?"

"But I didn't even know I made it."

"That's precisely why you were able to do it. You didn't think about it."

"Who are you?" he whispered.

"You know very well who I am. I'm your Traveler," said the woman. "My name is Meg. I've been waiting all my life for you to make a doorway for me. Finally you've come to your senses. Now, I'm going through that doorway, but I'll come back. I'll not lose you just when I've found you. Listen deep inside yourself while I'm gone. You'll be able to hear me."

She ran up to Asa and gave him a hug. "I know you feel bad, but you've done a wonderful thing. You've trapped the Provisioner," she said. "And you've finally been true to yourself. You made a doorway!"

Asa flinched and groaned in pain. He didn't care about the doorway. He cared only about getting to Talfassa.

"Oh, I'm sorry," said Meg, and dabbed at his bloody face with the edge of her sleeve. "Goodness, you're a mess." She shook her head. "You've hidden yourself for too long. You must be proud of who you are," she said fiercely. "We are a pair. We shall have a lifetime together. You won't be alone any longer. I'll be back." She turned and walked through the doorway. There was a faint sizzling sound, and she was gone.

She would not come back. Not for a very long time. And Asa would not reach out to her, for his newly found hope abandoned him that night for good.

Asa was soon heralded as a hero, the Provisioner's capture attributed to him. But he harbored a secret that ate away at him: He was a coward. He had been running *away* from the Provisioner.

He had wanted to jump into the Map himself, everybody else be damned! It was purely an accident that the Provisioner ended up trapped in it instead.

Asa was deeply ashamed. He retreated to Trout Island. He was determined to make himself forget Meg. He was not worthy of her; he was not worthy of anybody. He would close himself off to the world.

———————————

Asa shuddered and was brought back to the present. He took a handkerchief from his pocket and wiped his damp face. It overwhelmed him even now, the events of that night. He did not like to think of his Traveler. It produced an ache in him, an emptiness: a regret of a life not chosen.

He looked down at the Map. It had been years since he had looked at his creation. He had visited it many times during those first few months to see if it had begun breathing again, but the Map had never recovered. Every day it breathed a little less, until one day it simply stopped.

Asa traveled the Map slowly, his eyes sweeping from east to west, from north to south. There was the tiniest little ripple, so tiny it was almost a smudge, but as he examined it over and over again he realized what he was seeing. The Map was beginning to breathe again! He didn't think of how this might affect the Provisioner. His only thought was that after all these years, perhaps *now* he would be allowed to go to Talfassa. And so Asa stole it.

Chapter Five

It was June 15, the last day of sixth grade at Hazard School. The teacher had stepped out of the room for a moment. Kids were screaming, throwing Skittles at each other, smearing the chalkboard with finger paints someone had stolen from the first-grade shelf of the art-supply room. Billy sat quietly in the corner, peeling the frosting off a Hostess cupcake. He hated homemade cupcakes—they were always dry and got stuck in your throat. Store-bought were the best. Only one more afternoon, he told himself—a few more hours to get through. He laid out the frosting on a paper towel. He would save it for later.

Nobody paid any attention to Billy; they never had. A few weeks ago he had had some hope that things might change, that at the end of sixth grade his class might redeem itself, because his teacher had chosen him to lead the graduation ceremony. Billy daydreamed about being invited to some parties, being asked to play volleyball or go to Newport Creamery for an Awful-Awful milkshake after school. After all, it was an honor to lead the graduation. But it had only made things worse.

"Teacher's pet," the kids hissed at him. "Brownnoser. Suck-up. You smell like manure."

This was the worst insult, because to attack the way someone smelled was simply cruel. There was no witty reply to that kind of remark. What were you supposed to say—"No, I don't"? Billy also worried that it was true; there was always some kind of poop on his shoes from mucking out the barn.

Meg told him it was time to buck up and fight. "You're almost twelve now," she said. "Stand up for yourself."

That was easy for her to say. He still hadn't figured out how to do this. It certainly wouldn't be with his fists. Billy was the smallest kid in the class. He always wore long sleeves because his arms were the diameter of the lower end of a baseball bat. It was embarrassing. He tried never to be seen with his shirt off. Where was the teacher, anyway? he wondered as kids threw rolls of toilet paper at one another, practically on the floor hysterical with laughter. Billy didn't get it; he never had. What was so funny about toilet paper?

"Hey, Nolan, heads up!"

Somebody hurled a tennis racquet at him.

Before Billy had time to think, he shrieked "NO!" and threw his hands up. There was a sizzling sound. A window appeared in front of him. Billy swore, knowing what was about to happen. The tennis racquet sailed through the window and disappeared.

The classroom went absolutely silent. Billy lowered his hands and stared at them. Each palm was stamped with an identical pattern of squares within squares, and an eerie blue light was streaming out of them.

Everyone stared at him, horrified. Many of the kids were covering their mouths with their hands. Some were actually leaving, backing out the door as if he were contagious. Paul MacMahon screamed, and someone yelled for the teacher. Billy could hear his classmates' thoughts, and they pierced through him like knives. *Freak. Monster. Animal.* He covered his ears with his hands and ran.

*   *   *

When Billy opened his eyes, he was in the custodian's office, sprawled in the corner amidst the industrial-sized buckets of bleach and floor wax. The clock said it was 4:30. Billy groaned and sat up. He'd made it to the office and collapsed as an unfathomable exhaustion had overtaken him. He had been asleep here for nearly three hours.

Billy stood up and looked at his hands. He could see the faintest remnant of the pattern on his palms, but it was mostly gone. He was back to normal. The disappearance of the tennis racquet would be harder to explain. He would claim ignorance or fever. He would walk the other way when he saw anybody from his class this summer.

He'd better get home; Meg was probably frantic.

Billy let himself out of the empty building. He walked across the playground, looking carefully for signs of other kids. The concrete was deserted. What a way to end sixth grade! He knew he wouldn't come back for graduation.

He cut through the woods. It was only a mile home, and if it had been up to him he would have walked every day, but he had to take the bus because he was in elementary school. In a few years it would be different. People didn't care so much about you when you got older. You got less precious. Billy looked forward to this.

He walked through the fields and climbed the stairs to the back deck. He could see Meg on the phone, the cord laced through her fingers, the way it always was when she was nervous. He coughed. The screen door was open.

"Oh, thank God, he's here," she said to whomever she was talking to, and threw the phone down, her face crumpling with relief. She pulled him into the house.

* * *

Unlike Billy, Nora had had a very good last day of school at Waitsfield Elementary. Six weeks had passed since Nora and Billy had met. Billy looked just as he had that first day on Moonstone Beach— the same straight red hair, bangs that hung in his eyes, ears that stuck out in a funny way—but Nora was almost unrecognizable.

She had grown an inch and gained five pounds. Her ankles stuck out of all her pants; her mother had had to let the hems down on everything. Her hair had gotten longer and shinier. In short, Nora Sweetkale had become dazzling. All the sixth-graders at Waitsfield Elementary thought so.

How could we have passed her over? her classmates wondered, sifting through old school pictures and finding a small, unremarkable girl who for four straight years looked to the left of the camera as if someone were calling her. Nobody noticed her until one day she was just there, and everybody saw her at the same time. It was as though she had finally stood up after being seated for her entire life.

Nora credited the blue book with the remarkable changes in her life. She believed she was beginning to experience the payoff for her allegiance to it. The book made her feel as though she could do anything, be anybody. It made her feel she could be great.

Nora had started taking gymnastics at the YMCA. She was a natural. She was also a bit of a show-off. On the last day of sixth grade, she did ten back handsprings in a row through the middle of the schoolyard. Everyone grew silent when they heard the running that announced the beginning of her leap. Heads swiveled at the sound of her feet on the pavement. Her lean body moved effortlessly through the air, long legs scissored across the sky.

A group of girls gathered around Nora when she returned to earth. They were wild with excitement about being let out of school, chattering about swimming at the Guild, art classes, a trip to Block Island. Nora, her cheeks flushed with all the attention, the reality of her blossoming popularity taking root somewhere deep inside her, said yes to everything.

*   *   *

"Well, I've got gymnastics on Mondays, Wednesdays, and Fridays; painting on Tuesday mornings; and a standing date with Holly and Mary to meet every Thursday morning at the pool," Nora told Billy. She picked at a scab on her ankle, her long hair shielding her face.

"Suzy Q?" Billy asked breezily, carefully tearing open the cellophane with his teeth. If you were in too much of a hurry with Suzy Qs, you left half the chocolate cake on the cardboard.

He was trying to act nonchalant, as if Nora's news of her full summer schedule did not crush him. What had happened in the past six weeks? Billy had gotten weirder, more estranged from his peers, yet Nora had gotten more confident and popular. He didn't understand it. *He* was the one who could make the windows and doorways. *He* was the one who should be experiencing wonderful things as a result of his newfound powers. It didn't seem fair. He felt more apart from the world than ever.

"Nah," Nora said. "I've got to watch my weight."

"That's stupid," Billy snapped, unable to hide his annoyance and jealousy any longer. "Here." He handed her a Suzy Q. "Eat it," he commanded impatiently, suddenly feeling mean.

Nora did. They sat in silence for a while, licking the sticky cake from their fingers. They were both sad, but they couldn't say why. They felt as though they were talking from a great distance, even though they were sitting in the grass not more than a foot away from each other.

"So how about Monday, Wednesday, and Friday afternoons?" Nora offered softly. "I'm out of the gym by noon."

Billy nodded, grateful to her for reaching out to him.

"I think we've been going about it the wrong way," he said.

"What?" asked Nora.

"We should be trying to push through."

"Push through the windows?"

"Yeah."

"But they're windows, not doors."

"I'm not sure about that," said Billy. "I told you I thought there was another kind of opening, a door, but what if there's not? What if we're supposed to force our way through the window?"

Nora gave him a disgusted look. "Force our way through?"

Billy felt defensive. "What's the harm of experimenting?"

"There could be a lot of harm."

"Well, we've got nothing to lose," snapped Billy.

"I thought you said you could make a door," she said, frowning.

"I can!" cried Billy, two bright spots appearing on his cheeks.

"Okay, okay," said Nora. "Calm down. I didn't mean to get you upset." She reached over and put her hand on his shoulder. "It's a good idea. Let's try it."

And so they did.

They spent the last two weeks of June experimenting. They tried all sorts of different tactics to force their way through the windows Billy made. The windows always showed them the same thing: Asa Trout at the lilac cottage. Sometimes they saw Tria, sometimes not. They pressed down lightly on the window with just the palms of their hands. They tried to find the edge of the window and peel it back. They plunged a knife into the window and tried to rip it open, which did nothing but distort the scene. They even jammed a radio up against the window to see if Asa could hear into their world as they could hear into his, but he gave no sign that he did.

They were close; Billy could feel it. He wasn't really worried about his ability to make a door. He was more worried about losing Nora before it happened. As the weeks passed, it seemed she was pursued by everybody. Her mother, her other friends, her other interests—even that strange blue book in her knapsack—were constantly pulling at her. Billy knew they didn't have much time; he had to keep her focused on the task. He didn't know what the strange markings were that flickered on his palms or why he was able to make windows, but he knew one thing: He needed Nora's help. He could not do this alone.

Chapter Six

*T*hings were not going well on Trout Island. Now that the Map was there, Tria would no longer come inside the cottage. Asa came to believe her desertion was due to a combination of the Map being there and the fact that after he stole it he and Tria were spied upon quite regularly by the boy and girl.

Asa got used to ignoring the children, but Tria found it hard to do this. The children usually appeared for only a few minutes. They were always trying to get his attention, waving and screaming, but then they would blessedly disappear. It was too much for Tria to endure. Asa decided to make the doublecat a new home in the shed—anything to get in her good graces again.

He built her a loft. A mohair blanket lined her bed. Asa made her Potatoes Anna every evening and gave her bowls of lemon ice for dessert. Every week he fashioned a caramel lick, a large block of toffee he hung on a rafter that she could lick without even moving from her cushions. But it was not enough. Tria was a sensitive animal. Even from the shed she could feel the Map.

Asa knew the Map smelled bad to Tria. He could tell by the way she wrinkled her nose. And even though it was coming to life, each day breathing a bit more, Asa had to agree with her: Something about its recovery was off. Its breathing was labored; most of the time it sounded like it was suffocating, like somebody had a hand over its mouth. Then one day Asa saw the Provisioner staring out at him through the surface of the Map.

The Provisioner was watching him silently, the bridle and bit interlaced in its fingers. How long it had been watching him, Asa didn't know. He turned the Map to the wall, though he hated to do this; it was as if he were turning his back on a friend.

The Map's pitiful state continued to torment him. Every day its breath quickened, but Asa knew it was not quickening with health. The Provisioner was trying to force its way out.

Oh, how much pain Asa had caused! He could barely tolerate it. He felt he deserved to be left alone, and so he was. Tria was now gone all night. She'd return in the mornings for food, ill-groomed, her fur full of twigs, paws muddied. After a while she stopped coming back in the mornings and made appearances only now and then after dark. Then she was gone for days, even weeks at a time, and finally Asa stopped expecting her at all.

*   *   *

Three weeks had passed since Molly had decided the Map That Breathed would be the topic for her first Lifework. She had planned to go straight to the Remembery and inform Headmaster Sugg of her plans, but the very next day the Map had been stolen from Sanasarea Hall. How could she research it if it was nowhere to be found? Finally, after much deliberation, she decided to go along with her original plan. The mystery of the Map had only grown more complex, and she found this thrilling.

"So you've finally chosen," said Headmaster Sugg, looking at Molly Berry with contempt.

Molly was the last one in her class to decide on a topic for her Lifework. Headmaster Sugg had never liked her; he'd always found her arrogant. Here she was, one day before the due date for declaring a Lifework. The other students had decided upon their topics months before. He hoped he'd have the pleasure of flunking her.

Molly sat in his office, an overdone, ostentatious room. The Headmaster himself, whom Molly thought looked ridiculous in his self-assigned scarlet robes, wore rings on every finger and a golden book on a chain around his neck to signify his rank. He was a vain, silly man who trimmed his beard and mustache every day and was so worried about his breath he was constantly sucking on mints. He was right to worry; even through the mint Molly could smell the tooth rot. She tried not to grimace.

"It's about time. High grades are not enough," Headmaster Sugg berated her.

"I'm sure you feel that way," said Molly, looking up from the very uncomfortable chair the Headmaster had in his office, a chair whose sole purpose was to make its occupant squirm.

Headmaster Sugg looked at Molly with what he hoped was a bored expression. In truth Molly did anything but bore him; he was rather threatened by her. She was one of the most brilliant students to come through the Remembery in a long time. Years ago Dallan herself had asked to be kept abreast of Molly's progress. This made the Headmaster hate her.

"So, what is it? I have precious little time," snapped Sugg. "Do enlighten me as to the subject matter of your Lifework."

"I'm not prepared to tell you," said Molly. "I don't mean to offend you, sir"—this was a lie, she certainly did want him to take offense—"but I'd like to present my treatise to Dallan."

Headmaster Sugg looked at her with undisguised fury. She was well within her rights to request a hearing with Dallan, but to bypass him was an insult. He was livid and he was curious. Just what had the girl stumbled upon?

"Very well," he said, not having a choice in the matter. If her treatise was not of the highest potential, Dallan would send her back to him. He grinned, thinking of how he would make her suffer when she returned. "I'll set it up."

"Thank you, sir," said Molly, standing to go.

"One more thing," said the Headmaster. "You really think you're of the caliber to enter the Deeps?"

"I don't know, sir. I imagine the artifacts will let me know."

"They will indeed, my girl," he snapped. He had never been invited into the Deeps. "You're a cheeky sort."

"That I am, sir. My father says it's the only way to get things done."

"Tell your father he's wrong," he said, his confidence restored. The Berrys were a classless bunch, not worth his energy.

He waved his hand at Molly and turned toward his beloved artifacts, which sat on the highest shelves, well out of reach of any of the apprentices. The artifacts were objects from other worlds that

Travelers attending the Aquisto had unsuccessfully tried to bring back to Talfassa. Somehow these items got stuck in the Greenwater Veil. Eventually they dislodged and made their way to Sanasarea, where they were cleaned off and brought to the Remembery. The Headmaster had been given the simplest of these artifacts by Dallan, and he displayed them like priceless works of art. They were the only things that offered him solace. Nothing from his own world brought him such pleasure. The most valuable artifacts were in the Deeps, still awaiting a Rememberer to unlock their mysteries.

"How am I to know if Dallan will see me?" asked Molly.

"I'll send word to you," said Headmaster Sugg, annoyed the girl was still in his office. He turned his back on her again, signaling her dismissal.

*   *   *

Dallan, the oldest Rememberer alive, was in her room. It was a sunny, bright room, its walls lined with books. She could remain there for another lifetime and be satisfied, if only Headmaster Sugg would leave her alone. There was nothing that annoyed Dallan more than the sight of his fawning face. Especially that evening when she was ready to retire.

"Oh, what is it now?" she moaned, hearing his rap upon the door.

"There's been a request for a hearing, Madam," said Sugg. "I only come to tell you, as is my duty."

"Stop it, you idiot," said Dallan. "Enter and don't call me Madam."

Sugg walked into the dimly lit room. Dallan looked even tinier than usual, clad only in a deep purple nightgown. The old Rememberer wore nothing but purple for two reasons: one, it was a color reserved for esteemed elders, and two, it made her dark skin luminous. Sugg reddened in embarrassment—clearly she was about to go to bed.

"Well, who is it?" asked Dallan, although she knew very well who it was that had requested an audience. She had been waiting for years for Molly to approach her.

"Molly Berry."

Dallan nodded.

"Tell her I'll see her in a week's time. And ask her to bring some of her father's dulse relish," she said. Lou Berry made the most amazing condiments.

"You're not surprised?" asked Sugg, dismayed at how quickly she agreed to see the girl.

"Of course not," said Dallan. "I'm only surprised it's taken this long. Now, on your way, Sugg. I'm sure you've got plenty to attend to. Being Head of the Remembery is a full-time job. You must be up all hours of the night."

Headmaster Sugg bowed deeply, choosing to interpret her comment as a compliment, a testament to his dedication to his job, although it was anything but that. Dallan knew very well Sugg put in no more time than was necessary.

"You will let me know how I can be of help with the Berry girl, I trust," he said.

"You will not be needed," said Dallan. "Nor will you be informed. Go."

Dallan was 104 years old. She saw no need to be polite.

*   *   *

"Can't I go with you?" pleaded Roane. "I'm so bored with summer school. I promise I won't be a bother. I'll stay in the library. I'll read nicely. Please!"

Summer was the only time Roane got to see Molly. He missed her desperately during the year when they lived apart, she at the Remembery and he at the Growery. He couldn't bear to let her out of his sight.

Roane's dependence on her was grating. It was the last thing Molly needed. After a week she had finally gotten her audience with Dallan, and she didn't want Roane tagging along.

"You're seven years old," Molly scolded him. "Old enough to be on your own." She detached his hands from her skirt and stood up. "I'll be back at dinnertime."

The boy began to cry. "But I can't help it. I miss you so much."

Molly sighed deeply. He was such a tender boy. He needed to toughen up.

"Oh, Roane. Stop being such a baby. I'll be back in a few hours. Now buck up and get yourself to the Growery," she said in a harsh voice.

Roane's face crumpled, but Molly didn't allow herself to look back. She was late. She ran out the door.

*   *   *

"It's taken you a long time," said Dallan, studying the young woman who stood in front of her.

"I know," said Molly. "I was waiting for the right topic."

Molly was nervous. She stood in Dallan's room, a surprisingly welcoming place, colorful carpets scattered across the floor, a pot of tea brewing on the table. She was startled to see that Dallan was tiny, barely bigger than Roane. Although the old woman had a commanding voice, her black eyes were soft, and Molly let herself be comforted by this.

Someone else might have attributed the softness to a certain vulnerability that comes with age, but Molly knew better. Dallan's mind was exquisite, still so sharp she could drag you across it and draw blood. If asked, she could name every person ever born in Sanasarea and all their descendants. She could tell you the common name, family, habitat, and folkloric and medicinal uses of every weed, flower, and plant in all of Greenwater. She also knew many other, more esoteric facts that she never had the pleasure of sharing with anyone.

"That's not what I meant," said Dallan. "Why didn't you come see me long ago?"

Molly was bewildered. "I . . . I didn't know that was an option. I didn't know you saw people."

Dallan sighed. "I don't. Not many, anyway. But I would have seen you."

Molly blushed.

"You know you have what it takes?" Dallan asked. She thought she might as well get to the point.

"To do this Lifework?"

"To take my place when I'm gone," said Dallan. "I won't live much longer. Somebody will need to run the school."

"But Headmaster Sugg—" said Molly.

"Headmaster Sugg is a fool. He's a figurehead. I run the school, and you will after I'm gone."

Dallan watched the young woman grow pale. She knew this was not what Molly had expected. Molly wanted only to be let into the Deeps to do her research, not to be asked to take on such a huge responsibility.

"You don't have to worry," said Dallan. "There's not much to do. Well, there is, but it's only what comes naturally to you, so it won't be overwhelming. Sugg will continue to administrate. Your life will be spent in the Deeps, as mine has. To have a Remem-berer probing, learning, constantly advancing our understanding of our world in relation to other worlds, this is the lifeblood of the school. This is what keeps it going. Do you understand?"

Molly stared at Dallan, her eyes wide. She was only able to com-prehend one thing, that Dallan was going to let her into the Deeps.

"So you think I'm ready for the Deeps?"

"I have no idea if you're ready," said the old woman. "But we'll soon find out. It won't be easy. The books don't give up their information for free, and neither do the artifacts."

Molly chewed on her lip. A part of her wanted to run out of the room. Another part knew this was what she had been born for.

"Don't you want to know my topic?" she asked.

"I know it. Asa Trout and the Map That Breathed. What I don't know is why."

"Because it seems that after he made the Map, the will to live bled out of him. I saw him a few months ago, and he looked near death. Something's terribly wrong."

"And you want to help him?" asked Dallan. "Bring the poor man back to life?"

"Well, no, I want to figure out what happened. Why the Map did that to him," said Molly matter-of-factly.

"I see. And you think the Map did something to *him*? How interesting." Dallan was silent for a few moments. She looked out the window at the Greenwater Sea; her brow furrowed. Finally she spoke.

"Molly, it's clear you've been well trained as a Rememberer. You are to be commended. You have become a master researcher, a master of recitation and memorization. But I must warn you—if you go into the Deeps, it will require something altogether different of you. If you want to know what happened to Asa Trout and discover the origins of the Map That Breathed, you must master compassion."

"I don't understand," said Molly, confused and a little scared about what Dallan was asking of her. This was not her world, the world of emotions. As a Rememberer, Molly prized herself on her rationality, her ability to state the facts. What Dallan was asking went against everything she had been taught.

"You will," said Dallan, walking over to her bookshelf. She pointed up at a blue vase. "Would you mind getting that for me?"

Molly handed it to Dallan, who reached in and pulled out a large golden key. She waved it in front of the young woman's face.

"The key to the Deeps?" Molly gasped.

"The key to the larder," said the old Rememberer. "Sugg keeps it locked up. Let's go get a snack, shall we, and then I'll show you around."

*   *   *

Asa walked out the front door of his cottage. He was skinny as could be, flat-stomached and flat-footed. He slumped. He walked slowly and with no grace.

The screen door slammed shut, startling him, making a loud clapping noise before it gave a groan and fell entirely off its rusty hinges. It landed just inches away from his heels. Asa turned to look at his home.

The lilac cottage and its surroundings were in a terrible state of disrepair. Wild strawberries had taken over the gardens, choking the cosmos and daisies, the hollyhocks and calendula. The grass had not been cut in ages and was knee-high, full of chickweed and ticks and spider nests. Rats gorged themselves in the collapsed compost hut in full daylight, bold and unafraid, eggshells and fish skeletons dangling from their tiny hands.

Asa could barely bring himself to go inside the lilac cottage any longer. He had no stomach for it. He spent most of his days roaming the island. Only when it was dark would he return for a quick meal of whatever vegetable or meat hadn't rotted that could be fried up easily in the skillet. He never slept through the night.

Asa looked with dismay at the door. Painting he could put off, washing dishes, cutting the grass, but a door he would have to attend to; he didn't like the thought of being plagued by mosquitoes. He went to the shed to get his tools.

The repairs didn't take him long. It actually felt good to use his muscles. There was a time when he could do all these things without even thinking about it. Today, it took work. He had to mutter the directions out loud to himself, as if instructing someone else.

He made the last adjustments and oiled the hinges so that they would not make a noise when he opened and shut the door. Hope flickered inside him. He had accomplished something besides staying away. It was an achievement.

Asa heard a noise—the padding of a large paw on pine needles. Tria! He did not look up; he didn't want to scare her. Perhaps this would be a good day after all. He hadn't seen her in weeks.

He stood quietly, waiting. The doublecat stepped into the clearing. She looked past him, through the screen door at the Map, which even from fifty yards away Asa knew was trembling.

The blanket he had thrown on it, the one he draped over the Map every morning to try to hide it, fell. Asa cursed. Both he and Tria heard the soft *whoosh* of the fabric hitting the floor, and then the lapping of water that was not coming from down at the dock but from inside the lilac cottage—from *inside* the Map.

Tria ran off. Asa watched sadly as his dearest companion fled through the trees, her cherry fur matted with thistles and thorns. She was shabby and bedraggled, nothing like her former regal self.

Chapter Seven

It was the middle of July, and the air quivered with heat. Billy lay on the porch hammock, waiting for Nora to arrive. It seemed like he was always waiting for Nora lately. Today she was at the dentist's office getting her teeth cleaned.

Billy was unhappy with their progress. Well, he was unhappy with *his* progress. He still hadn't managed to make a door, and forcing their way through a window was clearly not working. Billy hadn't admitted it to Nora, but he was beginning to feel like a failure. Plus, his parents were acting suspicious, asking just what he and Nora were doing all day long, and the summer was half over. Things were not going as he had hoped.

Billy's bare arm dangled off the hammock. He was wearing a tank top, which accentuated the fact that he weighed a paltry eighty pounds, but he was too hot to care. He heard the drone of the tractor far off in the fields. The radio played softly in the kitchen.

"Ah, forget it," he muttered and rolled out of the hammock, his sneakered feet slapping the wooden floor. He went into the kitchen, got a handful of grapes and a Coke. He grabbed a piece of paper and a pen.

Nora,

    Hope your teeth feel minty clean. I couldn't wait any longer. See you tomorrow. Call first. I don't know if I'll be available. I have things to do.

                    Billy

He signed the note with what he hoped was an I-could-care-less flourish and slapped it on the table where she would be sure to find it. He walked into the hallway and paused for a moment. He wanted to imagine he was Nora entering and coming upon the note.

"Billy, I'm here," he whispered, and strode back into the kitchen. He looked around, calling out his own name again, "Billy, Billleee," feeling ashamed, but unable to help himself. Then he let his eyes fall on the table. "Oh, a note," he said softly.

He read it. It was perfect. Cold. Punishing. Billy wheeled around and left.

            *   *   *

He walked along the irrigation ditches, lulled by the sound of the cornstalks rustling against one another. It sounded like presents being opened. He walked into the corn. He knew this wasn't a smart thing. There were acres and acres of fields. At this time of year the plants were nearly six feet tall and easy to get lost in, but

Billy didn't care. He was angry at Nora for being busy, angry at his own limitations, angry at everyone.

It was cool in the corn. He had goose bumps. He walked for a very long time, and the field just went on and on. His legs felt tired. Yawning, he sat down. Just a short rest, he thought. He stretched out, arms and legs spread to accommodate the stalks. When he woke, he made a door. He had not been trying. He had not even been thinking about it. He simply made a door.

*　　*　　*

"Meet me tonight," Billy whispered to Nora on the phone. He sat in the pantry. Light from the kitchen slashed the shelves in geometric slices. He absentmindedly read labels as they talked: Borden's Sweetened Condensed Milk, Uncle Ben's Rice, Campbell's Cream of Potato Soup.

"Do I need anything?"

"Bring a flashlight. A sweater. And meet me by the shed."

Billy hung up. He could hear the television going in the living room, his father laughing, his mother's knitting needles clicking; comforting sounds. He looked out the window and could see nothing but the dark shadows of the trees and fields. He shivered. There was no moon this evening. He was glad he had remembered to tell Nora to bring a flashlight.

"I'm going to bed," he called out.

"What are you reading?" his mother shouted, after a brief silence. "Must be pretty good to miss Friday-night TV."

"It is," Billy said abruptly, to discourage any more conversation. "See you in the morning."

He went to his bedroom. An hour later, he crept down the stairs and out of the house.

*　　*　　*

Nora was sitting on the stone steps of the shed, waiting for him.

"Hi." Billy grinned, tossing his own flashlight from hand to hand.

The events of that morning were forgotten: Nora's tardiness, his nasty note. All the differences between them were for the moment gone.

"Hi, yourself." Nora stood up. "I'm so excited," she said, squeezing his arm. "And I'm sorry I was so late."

"No problem," replied Billy, feeling generous and important, rather like a modern-day Magellan. "Ready?"

Nora took a deep breath and nodded. "Let's go."

*　　*　　*

The door hung there in the middle of the field. Stalks of corn twined around it like mementos surrounding a mirror. Billy and Nora looked through. There was no lilac cottage, no Asa Trout, no ruby doublecat, no grove of alder trees, no Map. There was only a field of corn—identical to the one they were standing in.

"Where did Tria go?" asked Nora.

Billy shrugged. "I don't know."

They were silent for a while, registering what they were seeing.

"May as well be a world away," said Nora.

"It *is* a world away," Billy replied. "We can't forget that. We can't make the mistake of thinking it's the same."

83

Nora turned to him and kissed him quickly on the cheek. It was a fast peck, her lips barely moist. Still, Billy was shocked. She had never kissed him before.

"And you made it," she said. Her eyes glistened in the dark.

They had not discussed who would go through the door. Billy had already decided that they couldn't both go through. It wasn't safe. One of them needed to stay behind in case anything happened, and that somebody would be Nora. He had made the door, after all.

*   *   *

A week passed. Nora skipped gymnastics, telling her mother the gym was closed for renovations. Early each morning she went to Billy's, arriving just in time for breakfast. Meg started setting a place for her at the table.

"Morning," Billy crowed as Nora opened the screen door on Saturday morning.

"Hi, Nora," said Meg, a frying pan in her hand. "Sausage or bacon? Maple or blueberry syrup?"

"Sausage and maple, please," said Nora, pulling out a chair and sliding up to the table. Her heart felt like a loaf of bread just placed in the oven. It plumped up the moment she walked into the Nolans' kitchen. It was good to be expected.

Billy cut into a large stack of pancakes with his fork. He was singing under his breath. He pierced a sausage and stuck it into his mouth whole, grinning. Nora giggled.

"Well, you two sure are happy," remarked Billy's father, folding up his newspaper. "Nora, it's wonderful having you for breakfast every day, don't get me wrong, but what's going on that you're willing to miss gymnastics for?"

Billy gave her a warning look across the table.

"Just summer," said Nora, shrugging. She was such a good liar, thought Billy. She never gave anything away.

He saw Meg signal to his father to let it go.

"Yeah, Dad," he said, rising from the table. "Just summer." He scraped the remains of his breakfast into the garbage. Nora took her pancake, rolled it up, and folded it into her napkin.

"For later," she said, stuffing it in the bib pocket of her overalls.

"That's fine," said Meg. "Billy, we need to go to Zayres tonight to get you some sneakers. Nora, you're welcome to come. Don't forget."

*   *   *

That morning they finally understood what they had been hearing off in the distance beyond the door: It was the sound of water.

"It's an island," Nora cried. "That's it! An island of corn!"

"You're right," said Billy, for that was exactly the sound, water lapping up on a shore, and if they stuck their noses up to the doorway they could even smell it, the fragrance of sun on the sea.

"We'll need a boat." He turned to Nora, his eyes grave. "And we'll have to make it out of corn."

Billy didn't know how he knew this, but he did, and as soon as he said it he knew he was right. A canoe, a rowboat, a float; none of those things would do. It would have to be a special boat made of corn from *their* side of the doorway. He slid his Swiss army knife out of his pocket.

He and Nora worked all day. Billy's fingers knew what to do. He tried not to think too much, as thinking was not the way to make this boat; feeling was. A coracle was what he wanted to build, a small, round boat, like an oversized bird's nest. He felt the knowledge rise up in him. Instinctively he wanted to hold it back, because it was scary. It was like throwing up—you knew you would feel better after you did it, but you tried to hold it back anyway because it would stink to actually go through it. Billy moved past that. He moved into a place where there was only the corn and the knowledge of how to fashion it into a watertight vessel. He reached over and showed Nora.

"Like this," he instructed. "You have to keep your hands loose. Shake your wrists out. Now be quiet. Listen to the corn."

Eventually Nora got it, although it didn't come as naturally to her as it did to Billy. He knew exactly how to braid the stalks into a fabric that would not be penetrated by water. When they were done, a strange vessel sat in front of them.

"It's like a cradle," said Nora.

No more than three feet long, it was an oval bowl, just large enough for one person to sit in. It curved up at the edges and had a rim of butter and sugar corn, the ears placed end to end. The bottom of the boat was lined with corn silk.

Billy picked the boat up and lifted it above his head.

"It's light," he said. "Weighs practically nothing."

He was pleased that even he could pick it up easily. He had been worried that he wouldn't be able to. He set it back down, and it rocked on the ground in front of them.

"It's beautiful," he said, admiring it.

"It is," said Nora. "I can't believe we made it."

"You know what it means?" Billy looked at Nora solemnly. She nodded, and he said the words they both had been waiting for. "It's time to go through."

They decided they would meet that evening. Midnight at the shed.

* * *

Billy and Nora parted ways. Billy went to get sneakers with Meg and then out for a NY System wiener afterward. He had chili on his dog; Meg had sauerkraut. She told him a slew of new jokes. He laughed so hard, milk came spurting out of his nose.

Later that night he watched one TV show and then feigned sleepiness. Before he climbed the stairs to bed, he bussed both Meg and his father on the cheek. His father was surprised, but he pulled Billy into his arms for a quick hug.

"Love you, Dad," Billy croaked softly.

"You, too, Billy." His father kissed him on the top of the head and let him go. "Everything okay?" he asked when Billy had reached the door. Meg had laid down her knitting in her lap as if preparing for a talk. Oh, no, thought Billy. He was nowhere near as skilled a liar as Nora was.

"Sure," he said.

"Your mom and I worry sometimes," said his father.

"You don't need to worry. Everything's fine."

"You're getting along well with Nora?" asked Meg.

"Of course," Billy said. "I wouldn't hang out with her if I wasn't. Why are you guys asking me such strange questions?" He knew why: His parents suspected something.

"You can come to us with anything," Meg said. "You know that. It doesn't matter what. We would understand."

Billy nodded, moved by her invitation. To take Meg into his confidence would be wonderful. For a moment he thought about confessing everything: his ability to make windows, the doorway out in the cornfield, the strange blue markings that shimmered on the palms of his hands. Then he decided against it. This was his, this power. He would tell his parents after he had successfully gone through the doorway into Sanasarea and returned.

"You don't need to worry, Mom and Dad. It's been a good summer. I'm happy."

His father exchanged looks with his mother as if to say *See*, and Billy knew he had managed to calm their fears. Meg gave him a smile and picked up her knitting.

"Off with you, then," she said. "See you in the morning."

*   *   *

When Nora got home, it was nearly suppertime. She kicked off her sneakers in the mudroom and tried to open the kitchen door. It was locked. She pounded on it for a few minutes while searching around in her pockets for her key. Then she remembered. Her mother was working late. Nora was supposed to pick up David at preschool and bring him home.

Nora looked at her watch. It was after five. The school closed at four. She went tearing out the door, jumped on her bicycle, and sped up the road. By the time she got there, her mother's car was the only one in the parking lot. The playground was empty. Nora ran inside.

Her mother was apologizing profusely to the teacher. A teary-eyed David was in her arms.

"You forgot me," David wailed when he saw Nora. "I was waiting and waiting." He buried his head in his mother's shoulder.

Ms. Sweetkale finished up with the teacher and came toward Nora, her face contorted with anger. "Not a word," she said, walking briskly past her daughter as if she were a stranger. "I'll deal with you when we get home."

She drove David home, leaving Nora to ride her bicycle. Nora rode slowly down Ministerial Road, all the excitement of the day gone. She knew she was going to be in big trouble. This was not the first time she had messed up. She had made lots of mistakes over the past weeks, forgetting to clean the bathroom, not putting her clothes away, leaving the milk out all day. Things between her and her mother had been strained but tolerable. But forgetting to pick up David was the worst possible breach of her mother's trust. And Nora truly felt horrible about it. She adored David; she would never have abandoned him on purpose. It was just that they had finally made the door. But of course she couldn't explain any of that to her mother.

Nora turned onto the gravel driveway, parked her bike in the garage, and walked slowly into the kitchen where her mother was waiting for her.

"You're grounded," her mother said. "For an entire month. No more going to the Nolans' house, no more gymnastics, no more painting or swimming lessons. Forgetting David, how could you? I've let many things slide. Your attitude, your bad moods, your laziness around the house, your self-absorption, but this is unforgivable. He's a child. He's dependent on us. How could you do that?" She was yelling now. "You're twelve years old. You are a member of this family. I need to be able to count on you!"

Her mother went on and on, but Nora began to drift away. Everything her mother said was true. Her attitude *was* horrible; she *had* been self-absorbed. But it was not entirely her fault: She had the book to look after. She was pursuing her destiny, and what did her mother know about that? Her mother probably didn't even believe in destiny; that's why Nora hadn't confided in her.

Nora watched her mother's lips moving in her angry face and made a decision. She was leaving. She was going to sneak out of the house tonight and go through Billy's doorway to Sanasarea. She'd show her mother. Pauline would be sorry for treating her this way.

Nora agreed to the punishment her mother laid out for her, since she had no intention of being around to endure it. She spent the evening with David, trying to get him to forgive her, which didn't take long because he had a short memory. She tickled him until he lay on the carpet exhausted with joy, a tiny rope of drool on his cheek. She wiped the drool off with her finger, surprisingly not grossed out. There was no sound better in the world than her brother giggling. She fed him supper, popping the french fries into his mouth one at a time. He opened and shut it to receive them like a little sparrow.

Nora knew she had come to the end of something, and the beginning of something else, and there was no turning back. The house cooled off rapidly as she and her mother sat in the living room later that night.

"I haven't heard you bring up this father business in a while," her mom said, looking up from her book. "Does that mean you're over it?"

"I don't think I'll ever be over it," Nora said, the words coming out of her mouth before she could stop them. She could not have lied tonight, not with what she was about to do.

"I'm not sure how to respond to that," said her mother, bracing herself for another fight.

"You don't have to say anything," said Nora. "It's for me to figure out. And I will, believe me, I will."

Her mother looked at her, taking note of her feverishly bright eyes, her flushed cheeks, and wondered if she had been too harsh with Nora. No, she decided. Children needed firm limits.

"Go to bed, Nora," her mother said, exhausted. "It's been a long day for all of us."

Chapter Eight

"**W**hat's wrong?" asked Dallan. She and Molly stood in the Deeps, a large rectangular room just off the Remembery basement. Molly was disappointed. This was the Deeps? It was nothing but a glorified warehouse, a boiler room. There was a huge pile of artifacts on the floor. They looked as though they had been thrown there with no thought or care. The artifacts were dusty and salt-encrusted. The room smelled moldy. All her life she had been waiting for *this*?

"You were expecting, perhaps, magic?"

"I was expecting more than this!" Molly cried, well aware she sounded like a whiny little girl. "Why, I can barely see!" The room was dark; she couldn't see past the pile on the floor. "Why didn't you bring a lantern?" She turned to Dallan.

"A lantern would be of no use. You can barely see because you don't know how to look. Not yet anyway, but you will learn," said Dallan calmly.

"This place is hideous!" Molly wrinkled her nose. "You need a charwoman, not a Rememberer."

"I need you, Molly Berry," said the old woman. She frowned. "I had expected you to be farther along than this, but nothing is ever as it appears. Very well, I'll give you a bit of what you crave."

She walked into the shadows, trailing her hand along the wall. In a moment the entire room was bathed in a soft plum-colored light. Molly saw that the ceiling was much higher than she had originally thought. On the left side of the room, hundreds of small alcoves were built into the wall, and in each was an artifact, but these were not dirty and salt-encrusted; they were burnished and glowing. Some of them were identifiable. There was a tusk, a bow and arrow, a figurine of a bull, a strand of bells, a blindfold, an amulet, a tiny ark. Other artifacts were clearly foreign: a large metal box with buttons and dials on the bottom, a small gray rectangle with numbers. Then there were things that made Molly shiver. An apron made out of bones. A halo that quivered as if it were alive. A roll of liquid bandages. Pressed into the back of each alcove was an almond-shaped stone that gave off the plum-colored light. The artifacts were displayed like works of art.

"The stone is called almandine," said Dallan. "It gives off a lovely glow, doesn't it?"

The back wall of the Deeps was a library. The shelving ran floor to ceiling, stuffed with books big and small, and on the right side of the room were the neat rows of alcoves again, but these were empty, waiting to be filled.

Molly bowed her head in shame as she saw Dallan's work in front of her. It must have taken her years to sort through these artifacts, understand their purpose, bring them back to life.

"I'm so sorry," she whispered.

"Don't be," said Dallan. "I reacted the same way when I first came down to the Deeps. It's an ugly, uninspiring place until you put yourself into it. You must learn patience. You must learn to see below the surface. That will be your task now, Molly Berry."

The door behind them opened as somebody or something butted against it. Molly gave a small shriek.

"Oh, it's just the lovelies," crooned Dallan as a family of double-cats strolled into the Deeps. The mother was emerald-colored, the father orange, and the three kittens were crimson, royal blue, and yellow. They sniffed around Molly disdainfully.

"It's all right, lovelies," Dallan said. "This is Molly. She'll be here now." She turned to the young woman. "They live here. They'll keep you company. You should bring them a treat whenever you come."

"I prefer to be alone," said Molly coldly. "I work best on my own with no disruptions."

"Mmm," said Dallan. "Too bad. I shouldn't think that method will be working for you much longer. Besides, the lovelies have always been here, haven't you, dears?" She scratched the doublecat mother under her green chin. "Cod, they prefer cod, remember that."

She clapped her hands together. "So, there's much to do, as you can see." Dallan gestured to the pile on the floor. "I suggest you start at the top and work your way down." She turned to go.

"Wait!" cried Molly desperately. "But what am I supposed to do? How does it work?"

"How does what work?"

"Where do I start?"

"Why, at the beginning, of course."

"But what's the beginning?" moaned Molly in dismay, realizing that she was on her own. Dallan was not going to offer her much in the way of instruction.

"Goodness, my girl. Have they taught you nothing? I'll have to talk to Sugg," said Dallan.

"Asa Trout, the Map That Breathed," Molly reminded her. Perhaps the old woman suffered from some sort of senility.

"Oh, right, right," said Dallan, shuffling back into the Deeps. "You'd like a little help with that, would you?"

"Yes, please," said Molly humbly.

Dallan walked to the back of the room, muttering to herself. "It was not a book . . . ," she mumbled, running her fingers absent-mindedly over the leather spines. "Not a manuscript, either, but something like that. Something smaller. A chart? No. A ledger? No, that's not it, either." Her hands alighted upon a rolled-up piece of parchment bound with a leather cord. "Aha!" she cried. She brought it over to Molly and placed it solemnly in her hands. "Here you are, my dear."

"What's this?" asked Molly.

"A scroll, of course. It came with the Map."

Molly's eyes lit up with excitement. Her blood began to thunder and her belly to roil. This always happened to her when she was in the presence of something powerful. The scroll was very old, perhaps even ancient. The edges of the parchment were buttery soft, worn with age. She walked over to the table, feeling rather breathless. She untied the leather cord and slowly spread the scroll wide with her hands. It was written in a foreign language. "But I can't translate this!" she cried.

"Neither can I," said Dallan. "But you will."

*   *   *

Dallan left Molly in the Deeps to sort it out. She could have told her more. She could have said that she was the one who had brought the Map to the tower room and left it there, for Dallan liked to stir things up. But she did not share this information with Molly. She wanted to see what the young woman came up with on her own. Dallan herself had no idea about the origins of the Map, and she was hoping Molly would be able to crack its code. It had eluded her for years.

*   *   *

Molly stayed in the Deeps until the following morning. She tried all her techniques, applied all her methodologies, everything she had been taught as a Rememberer. Her knowledge was wide-ranging and far-reaching. She had a brilliant mind that had been trained to contort itself, to squeeze into tight places, to metamorphose and shape-shift. She tried sorting, classifying, analyzing, insisting the language reveal itself to her. None of it worked.

She began to sift through the pile of artifacts, laying her hands upon each thing. She tried to bypass her mind, to reach more deeply inside herself. What was it that Dallan said would be required of her? Patience. Seeing below the surface. Compassion. Exactly the kinds of things she disdained. They were better left for somebody attending the Oraclery or the Beautery, not a scholar like herself.

After twenty-four hours had passed, a frustrated Molly finally left the Deeps. She rowed home to Berry Island wearily and went to bed immediately. Her father brought her up a bowl of pea soup and some toast and half a glass of ginger beer.

"It'll settle your stomach," he told her, holding the glass up to her lips. She managed a few sips and a bite of toast.

"Do you think you're ready for this?" her father asked. "You can always change your mind. Do something easier."

Molly shook her head. "I can't quit."

"I know you can't, Mol," he said. "Good for you."

Her father left. A few minutes later, she heard him plucking the strings of his harp. Then he serenaded her. He did all her old favorites. Finally Molly fell asleep. When she woke that afternoon, Roane was nestled under her arm, snoring noisily. He often sneaked into bed with her like this. She never seemed to mind in her sleep, but once she woke, it was uncomfortable to have somebody so close. It was hot; the room was stuffy. Molly slipped her arm out from beneath Roane, got up, and opened a window.

*   *   *

The day lost its bones and went slack. Molly didn't know what to do with herself. She felt heavy with despair at the task in front of her. She spent most of the afternoon sitting in her chair and looking off into nowhere. Once evening fell, her father and Roane packed the boat with blankets, lanterns, and musical instruments, the accoutrements of a typical summer evening. There was a barbecue and dance on Camarata, but Molly could not be convinced to go. The last thing she felt like doing was pretending to be jolly. She watched from the shore of Berry Island as all of Sanasarea sailed past her and converged on Camarata for the evening's event.

The Sanasarea Best Interest Council, believing that it held the best interests of the citizens of Sanasarea in mind, roasted a pig and dug a pit in which potatoes and corn bread baked. Giant bowls of sauce sat on a table for communal dunking of meat so moist and juicy it slid off the bone.

The festival went on long into the night. People had too much to drink. The vats of apricot ale were emptied and filled again. People ate, drank, and danced; they swung each other around wildly. Cots were set up on Sanasarea Plaza for those who decided to stay. The fountain made a nice lulling sound, and the younger children were brought there when they fell asleep. It was nearly midnight when Roane was carried there by his father. Lou Berry found an empty bed and peeled the young boy off his shoulder.

"Like a sack of potatoes," he said affectionately, placing Roane carefully in the bed, trying not to wake him up.

He kissed his son on the forehead. Still asleep, Roane tucked his hands under his belly and rolled over, and Lou went back to the dance.

*   *   *

Asa sat on the shore of Trout Island and looked across the water. Camarata was lit up and glowing. Laughter drifted across the water and made him feel as though it had hands and was grabbing him around the throat. He saw the torches burning on the pier, smelled the pungent wood smoke from the bonfire. He even heard the strumming of guitars and the joyful sounds of a fiddle. Never had he felt so alone.

Hooting and clapping carried over to him. Ah, they would be dancing now. The Sanasarea Waltz. Asa stood up and moved in time to the faraway music. He knew the song well. A dip, dip here, a bow and a shuffle there.

"Sanasarea, our island home. Never far, will we roam."

Asa sang softly under his breath. His knees ached. His back was stooped. He had turned thirty-one the day before.

*　　*　　*

The lilac cottage was empty. Dishes were piled high on the counter. Mice nibbled crusts, and a raccoon hopped up on the kitchen table. Without warning, the Map flew off the kitchen wall and soared across the room as if somebody had hurled it. Then it crashed to the floor.

It was a stunning sight—the miniature world of Talfassa was fully alive and breathing. For one moment it was there in all its glory. Then the image shattered as a hand swam up from the depths of the Map. The Provisioner pulled itself up and out of the Map like someone getting out of a pool, then scuttled across the kitchen floor like a spider.

The Map began writhing as if it were in pain. Crimson paint seeped out like blood and ran in rivulets onto the floor. In seconds it was over. The Map was dead. No one would ever have suspected that once it had breathed.

The sounds of laughter and merrymaking drifted in through the windows of the cottage. The Provisioner lifted its head and its nose twitched as it sniffed the air—the unmistakable smell of sleeping children.

The Provisioner went down to the sea.

*　　*　　*

The next morning the bell started ringing in the plaza before most Sanasareans were even awake. The bell hadn't been rung in years. It sounded only during emergencies, and it required immediate response. It was a deep, penetrating *dong, dong, dong* that pealed for miles, reaching even Fortune Island, farthest away from Camarata.

People climbed out of their beds and, still in their pajamas, piled into their boats. It was so early that everyone's breath steamed. The sun had not even risen above the trees. Mothers hustled their children into sweaters. Plum muffins and salmon cakes were distributed. Everyone ate soberly. There was no quarreling, but plenty of eye-rubbing and hair-smoothing went on. Babies slept, swaddled in blankets.

Eilon's Way was bustling. Boats moved in an orderly fashion, cutting a silent swath through the channel. Men nodded at one another in the quiet way men do during times of crisis. Children looked out at their classmates with big eyes.

From her boat Molly could see that an enormous circle of Sanasareans had formed on the plaza. It was an odd sight. Everyone wore slippers or was barefoot. Hair was loose and a-muss. Molly rowed her boat into a slip, tied up, and ran down the dock. People moved aside to let her pass, whispering behind their hands.

She didn't understand what was happening, why everyone was looking at her so strangely. Had word gotten out that she had been let into the Deeps? Was this some sort of a celebration to honor her? She felt herself blushing as the crowd parted to let her into the center of the circle. There she saw her father, on his knees, holding a limp Roane in his arms. Roane's face was slack. It had collapsed as if something had sucked the life out of him. Molly's eyes widened in horror.

Chapter Nine

*T*hings were not going at all the way Billy expected.

"But I'm the one who's supposed to go through," he argued.

"Who says?" snapped Nora.

"*I* made it."

"So what? I've been with you all this time."

"Without me, there'd be no door."

Nora was silent. It was true. Billy knew he had her.

He tore open a bag of cheese popcorn. He didn't offer any to Nora. She stared at him gloomily. Miserable, this whole business was, but Billy stood his ground.

"Why can't we both go through?" Nora whined for the umpteenth time.

"Because. I've told you already. I don't think it's safe for us both to go. Somebody has to stay behind in case something goes wrong."

"And how do you know that?" she demanded.

Billy shrugged. "I just know it."

Nora sighed and stuck out her hand. Billy shook some popcorn into it. He knew it would help. Meg always gave him crunchy food when he was in a bad mood.

"All right," she finally conceded. "Let's get it over with. We've been here nearly half the night." She stood up and wiped her cheesy hands on her jeans with loud slaps. "So what do you want me to do?"

Billy put on his knapsack, a bit ashamed that he had coerced Nora into letting him be the one to go, but in a second he was over it. He deserved to go; he was the chosen one. The knapsack was heavy. He had packed carefully, not knowing how long he'd be gone or what he might need in Sanasarea.

"What have you got in there?" Nora asked.

"Just stuff." He wasn't about to tell her what *was* in there: his well-worn copy of *Zippy the Chimp* (he had a thing for primates), pajamas, a tube of Tom's of Maine Spearmint toothpaste, a cassette of Paul McCartney and Wings' *Band on the Run,* and Meg's Secret deodorant—he had just started to get B.O. and didn't want to offend anybody in the other world.

"Helpful things, I hope. Things besides Good and Plentys and caramels?" Nora rolled her eyes. "First-aid kit, binoculars, a rain jacket, flares?"

She was so practical. He ignored her comment and took a deep breath.

"Okay, I'm ready."

Nora shuffled her feet nervously. "So you're just going to step through?"

"Yes, I'm just going to step through. But first the corn boat."

Nora helped Billy drag it in front of the door. "One, two, three!" they counted. The corn boat sailed through the door. Billy and Nora peered through and saw it settle on the other side. It bounced a few times and was still.

"Well, I'm off, I guess." Billy did a few deep knee bends and awkwardly touched his fingertips to his feet. All his joints creaked; an athlete he was not. He was, however, good in water. Arms pointed in front of him, he dived, only to find something, *someone*, pulling him back.

"Nora!" he screamed. He fell to the ground with a cry, and everything went black.

Nora did not intend to hurt Billy, only to get him out of the way so that she could get through the doorway first. But he fell to the ground, hitting his head hard. So hard he had passed out.

Nora sat with him for a few moments, feeling sorry for what she had done. Billy had a large bump on his head. She stroked his temple like her mother did for her when she was sick. Meanwhile the door shimmered in front of her.

She carefully shifted Billy's head from her lap to the ground. She picked up Billy's knapsack—in her excitement she hadn't thought to pack a bag of her own. All she had with her was a small purse, which held the blue book. She stuffed the purse into Billy's knapsack, then slid it over her shoulder.

"I can't believe I'm going to do this," she whispered, but she knew she was; she had always been the one meant to go through, not Billy.

Nora took a deep breath and stepped through the door.

*   *   *

Nothing was as she imagined it would be. She had no time to look around, no time to take in her surroundings, because the moment she stepped through, a bridle was slipped over her head.

Nora's mouth was wrenched open and a piece of metal shoved in that pulled her lips back from her teeth. The metal made a horrible clacking sound, and she gagged over and over again. She tossed her head trying to get the metal thing out, but it was attached to the bridle, and then she realized what the metal was. It was a bit, a bit so cold it was nearly frozen, and it burned her lips and tongue. She began to scream.

Part Two

Chapter Ten

*T*here was a homeless man in Waitsfield who had not spoken for many, many years. He passed the days in a sort of waking slumber and because of this had been nicknamed Rip. It was an apt name, for a Rip Van Winkle he was, stuck in a netherworld of waiting. Nobody knew what he was waiting for. Nobody cared. The homeless who lived in the abandoned fairgrounds west of Waitsfield were used to the sight of someone staring vacantly off into space. So Rip was left alone, day after day, year after year, until one summer night—the night Nora Sweetkale left Waitsfield and the Provisioner arrived—Rip woke up and began to weep.

He cried silently at first, his shoulders heaving up and down, his enormous hands covering his face. Soon his beard was drenched, and it was then that sound erupted out of him, sound that had been held deep inside him for 4,383 days.

Everyone in the homeless camp awoke, crept out from beneath tattered blankets, and formed a circle around Rip. It was not a gesture of love, but of solidarity. They watched Rip taking huge gulps of air, getting used to the atmosphere of the living once again.

"Breathe," somebody said, and they took it up like a chant, a song.

Long into the night they stayed, reminding Rip to breathe, until the giant of a man was emptied, his clothes soaked, his face soft; until it was clear something had ended and something else had begun.

Chapter Eleven

The next day at dusk, Asa went down to the shore for a swim. He was deeply worried. Late last night he had discovered the shattered Map. He knew the Provisioner had made its escape, and he had no idea what he was going to do about it. Part of him thought he should immediately confess: go directly to Camarata, call a meeting of the Best Interest Council, warn everybody, tell them his Map had not been able to hold the Provisioner after all. Another part of him wanted to continue hiding, hoping the entire mess would simply vanish and go away.

Asa was waist-deep in the sea before he noticed the boat bobbing toward him from the direction of Corn Island. It wasn't until the boat was ten feet away that he realized it was made out of corn, and it wasn't until the boat was directly in front of him that he saw the girl curled up in the bottom of it. She was asleep.

Asa studied her. There was no mistaking it: This was the Traveler who had been spying on him through the windows in the aspen grove. Something had happened to her. Her hands were clenched into tight fists. The corners of her mouth were cracked and bleeding. Asa had a horrible feeling this had something to do with the Provisioner.

He dragged the boat onto the shore. He poked the girl and tried to awaken her. She did not stir. But her deep slumber seemed natural; she didn't appear to be stripped of her soul. He lifted her carefully and carried her to the lilac cottage, where he placed her in the circular alcove bed that had been Tria's before he brought the Map home. He covered her with blankets and laid her knapsack at the foot of the bed.

That evening Asa picked up what was left of the Map and brought it to the shed. Pieces of the canvas were ripped from the frame. Two of the egg-sized jewels had popped out. Once a relic, a near-holy object full of grace and power, the Map was now destroyed. He tried to restore it, smoothing the pieces of the canvas back into place, but soon realized it was useless. He covered the Map with an old blanket and went back to the cottage to check on the girl. She was still sleeping. Asa climbed into his boat and rowed to the island of corn; he needed to find out what had happened.

It was not a pleasurable ride. The water was not clear and luminous as it usually was; it was thick and oily and coated his oars like a skin. The skies were heavy, thunder threatened, and there was the smell of sulfur and mudflats in the air even though it was high tide. Asa forced himself to keep rowing. When he got to the island the stench was overwhelming, and he realized it was not just sulfur that he was smelling. It was the smell of stolen souls, of hatred, of fear, and he knew the girl and the Provisioner had been on this island a short time ago.

Asa's hands were searing hot. He didn't have to turn them

over to know the Kapth were becoming more pronounced, as if someone were carving the patterns into his flesh with a knife. He walked to the center of the island and found the doorway the girl had traveled through into Sanasarea. He peered through the doorway and saw an identical field of corn. It was a fabulous door, barely discernible; this was the work of a master. He would never have thought the redheaded boy capable of it.

"Brilliant," Asa muttered with admiration.

Suddenly he knew what had happened, or rather what he hoped had happened: The Provisioner had walked through this doorway into the girl's world. He felt a pang of guilt that the Provisioner roamed free in another world, preying upon other children, but he did not allow those thoughts to linger. Instead he focused on the doorway. Seeing it affected Asa profoundly. Another Gatemaker had made this door, not him, but the sight of it filled him with excitement. The girl must have come to him for a reason. Asa turned his hands over as the Kapth glowed up at him with a soft blue light, and he saw for the first time the beauty in what he had always considered his deformity.

*   *   *

Molly stood in the middle of the pile of artifacts. She had been in the Deeps for nearly twenty-four hours straight. She felt as if she would drop from fatigue and anguish. What kind of a sister was she? Roane had begged her to take him with her, begged her to spend time with him. But she had been cold. She had been harsh. She had treated him like a stranger, and now he was gone.

Molly grabbed a bottle filled with dark green powder. She sprinkled the substance into the air. She put a bit of it on her tongue. She rubbed it between her fingers. Nothing. She leapt off the pile of artifacts and began to hammer the bottle against the wooden floor.

"Reveal yourself!" she screamed in frustration.

The artifact remained stubbornly itself and did not shatter. Neither did it give any sign of life. Molly had no sudden insights into its purpose. She laid her head on the ground and began to sob. She sobbed until she fell asleep, and then she slept deeply and fully, as she hadn't slept for many years, since she had been a child.

Molly awoke to the clover-colored mother doublecat licking her ear. It wasn't an unpleasant feeling; in fact it was rather comforting. She opened her eyes to see five giant jewel-colored feline faces peering down at her.

"Did you bring them cod?"

She sat up. Dallan stood in the doorway of the Deeps.

"What?" Molly struggled to wipe the sleep out of her eyes.

"Cod. You must have. They've already become attached to you," said the old Rememberer, noting the way the lovelies crowded around the girl in a protective fashion.

Molly shook her head. "I haven't brought them anything."

Dallan raised her eyebrows. Doublecats were mercenary creatures. She had never known them to bestow their favors upon humans who did not extend themselves first.

"Nonetheless, they've claimed you. They've made you one of their family."

"I have a family," snapped Molly.

"So you do, Molly Berry. Although you haven't always acted as though you did," said the old woman softly.

Molly got to her feet, despair clouding her features. What Dallan said was true. She was ashamed.

"Have you had any luck?" asked Dallan, her eyes roaming the Deeps, noting the books left open on the table, pages torn out, bindings stretched. She frowned. This was no way to treat these priceless items. They would never reveal their secrets if they were not handled with respect.

Molly shook her head angrily. "They won't tell me anything!"

"And what is it that you want to know?" asked Dallan.

"How to save Roane! How to bring him back to life!" Molly cried.

"And what of Asa Trout and the Map That Breathed? You're dropping that?"

Molly stared at her in shock. "Of course I'm dropping it. Everything's changed. Roane's soul has been stolen by the Provisioner. I've got to find a way to help him!"

Dallan sighed. "Oh, dear girl, you've got a long way to go. The two subjects are likely related, as everything is in this world."

"I don't understand," moaned Molly. "You're talking in riddles. Just tell me what you mean."

"Your work is still the same. You cannot force the artifacts or the books. You must learn to move deeper inside yourself. To use the three hundred different colors that exist in your palette instead of only the ten you know so well."

Molly looked at her wearily.

"Go," said Dallan, clumsily attempting to draw the girl under her arm, which was an impossible task, as Molly was much taller than she was. She finally just took Molly's hand and patted it.

"Go home to your father, comfort him," she instructed. "Go to Roane and sit with him. It's all the boy's ever wanted, isn't it? Your undivided attention? Now give it to him."

Molly nodded miserably and let Dallan lead her out of the basement. The old woman was a compass, and how Molly ached for true north.

*   *   *

Late that night, Dallan sat up in her bed, unable to sleep. She knew the Provisioner was no longer in Sanasarea. She could not smell it, she could not sense it. It had stolen Roane's soul and then disappeared. This should have been good news—no more Sanasarean children would be in danger—but Dallan feared it was not. She suspected this was only the beginning of something even worse. She could not help feeling a larger, much more dangerous presence had been awakened.

Chapter Twelve

When Billy woke in the cornfield, it was morning. Nora and his knapsack were gone. She had traveled through the doorway without him. Worse yet, she had stopped him from going through; she had thrown him to the ground. How could he have been so stupid? It had probably been her plan all along.

Billy stared at the doorway anxiously. It shimmered, taunting him. So what if she went through first. He stood up. He rocked back and forth on his heels. "One, two, three," he called out, feeling sick to his stomach, readying himself to plunge through. He did this ten times before he understood he could not bring himself to do it. He was too scared. Defeated, he set out for home.

*   *   *

The back door was wide open. Billy stood in the doorway, listening carefully, not knowing what to tell his parents, unsure of what they knew. Should he tell the truth or should he lie? He and Nora had been gone all night. He looked at the kitchen clock. It was ten in the morning. Surely they had noticed his disappearance. Surely Nora's mother had noticed she was gone. Billy heard the soft murmur of his parents' voices in the living room. He had no idea what to say to them. It turned out he didn't have to say anything.

When he entered the living room, his mother began crying. She stood up and walked toward him briskly with the strangest look on her face, a mixture of concern, relief, and something else Billy couldn't identify. The look terrified him. His mother had never hit him, but Billy thought that she was about to. He flinched involuntarily as Meg pulled him into her arms and hugged him fiercely.

"I'm so sorry," she whispered into Billy's ear. "We've underestimated you. I'm afraid we've made a dreadful mistake."

"What are you talking about?" Billy was confused. He pushed his mother away from him so that he could search her face. He saw that he had misread her. She felt guilty for something, not angry.

"Nora's gone," said Meg dully. It was not a question. It was a statement.

Billy looked over his shoulder at his father, who was standing by the bay window.

"The police just left," he said. "They'll be back shortly. Ms. Sweetkale reported Nora missing last night. She told them to come here."

"What do they think?" asked Billy.

"They think she was with you," said his father.

"She was, wasn't she?" asked Meg.

Billy nodded.

"You made a doorway," said Meg.

Billy looked at his mother, shocked. "You know about doorways?" he whispered.

"I know about windows, I know about doorways, and I know about Sanasarea," said Meg softly. "I only wish I had told you what I know sooner."

"I don't understand," said Billy, looking back and forth between his parents. "How could you know?"

Meg sighed. "You made a doorway out in the corn, right?"

Billy looked at his feet.

"Nora didn't wander off; she went through the doorway, didn't she?"

"Yes," Billy murmured.

"I see," said Meg. "I thought it was something like that."

"You've made doors, too, haven't you?" Billy asked, his excitement building.

Meg shook her head. "No. Listen to me. There are two kinds of people involved with doors. One is a Gatemaker, that's what you are. Do you know what that means? Have you guessed?"

Billy nodded again.

"Yes, of course you know. You make doorways between worlds. That's what a Gatemaker does."

"But how do *you* know that?" asked Billy.

Meg was silent for a moment. She looked as if she were weighing something. "The other kind of person involved with doors is called a Traveler. Nora is a Traveler."

"That's why Nora went through?" Billy asked.

"Precisely. It was her destiny to travel through the door. It was yours to make it."

"And how do you know that?" Billy asked again, trembling, not sure if he wanted to hear his mother's answer.

"Because I'm a Traveler, too, and I went through a doorway my Gatemaker made when I was a young woman."

"You mean you went into another world?" asked Billy, astounded. "Like Nora did?"

"Yes," said Meg slowly. "Like Nora, I went into another world, only the *other world* I went into was this one."

"You're not from here?" asked Billy, his voice shaking.

"No, Billy. I'm from Sanasarea."

"When did you come here?"

"When I was twenty-two."

"And you never went back."

Meg shook her head.

"Why not?"

"I guess it was my destiny to come here. Just as it was yours to make the doorway out in the corn and Nora's to go through it."

Billy was flabbergasted. His knees felt wobbly. He thought he might faint. He turned to his father.

"Are you from Greenwater too?"

"No, I'm from Waitsfield," his father said gently.

Billy tried to take all this in. He felt strangely betrayed.

"Well, does Dad know you're not from here?" Billy shouted at his mother.

"Of course he knows! How could I keep that from him?"

"But you kept it from me!" Billy cried.

His mother and father looked at each other, worried.

"We had no idea you were so advanced, Billy. We thought you

were just fooling around with the windows. We didn't think you'd be capable of making a doorway for years," explained Meg.

"But I did," said Billy grimly.

"You did, and Nora's gone," said Meg. "And there will be repercussions now. Do you understand? Repercussions."

"She'll come back," said Billy.

"We don't know that," said Billy's father. "Your mother didn't go back to Sanasarea. And Nora's already been reported missing." He looked out the window nervously. "We don't have much time. The police will be coming back, and you're here. We've got to come up with a story. Now."

Billy wasn't ready to come up with a story. He was still reeling from learning that his mother was from Sanasarea.

"So this means I'm half Greenwater?" he asked.

"Yes, and half of this world," said Meg.

"No wonder I'm such a weirdo!"

"You're not a weirdo! You are gifted, and you are just beginning to understand the power of your gifts, Billy," said Meg.

"Well, what if I don't want those gifts?"

Meg frowned. "I don't think you have a choice."

Tears welled up in Billy's eyes, and his throat felt like it was stuffed with cotton. "I want to know everything," he implored. "You've got to tell me everything about Greenwater."

"There's no time for that," said his father as a police cruiser pulled into the driveway.

*   *   *

Neither his mother nor father said a word as they tramped through the corn. Billy was terrified now that he knew what was at stake.

"So tell us what happened." His father pretended that he was just hearing Billy's explanation for the first time.

"We thought we'd camp out in the corn," said Billy, his voice trembling, deciding to stick to the simplest of stories. He had no idea what would happen when he brought them to the doorway. Would the police be able to see it? Would his parents? Would it still be there? Billy tried to probe the minds of the police officers. He found their heads jammed with protocol. He had to move all that aside before he could get to their emotions. The older policeman was relatively empty. He was just doing his job, but the younger police officer was nervous. This was his first major case. Hmm, Billy thought, this information might come in handy.

"Why? Why in the world would you want to do that?" his father bellowed, putting on a show for the police, the stern father.

"I don't know. We just thought it'd be fun." Billy knew he had to play dumb. Act like a normal kid.

"This is it. Where we were, I mean," Billy said.

They had arrived at the doorway. It was still there. Meg could see it. Her eyes gave her away, filled as they were with a strange light. She seemed exhilarated and scared. His father saw nothing; neither did the two policemen. Billy was relieved.

"And you brought no tent? No sleeping bags?" the younger policeman asked, walking around the area of trampled corn carefully. He had introduced himself as Officer Monday.

"No, sir."

"Doesn't sound like much of a campout to me," said Officer Monday. "No snacks, no flashlight, no deck of cards? You brought nothing?"

"Well, I had my knapsack." As soon as Billy said this, he knew he shouldn't have.

"Your knapsack? So where is it?" asked the young officer.

The older policeman was examining bent stalks of corn, looking for evidence or something, Billy thought. He wondered if they could fingerprint corn.

He could not think of another lie, so he told the truth. "I don't know. When I woke up it was gone. Maybe Nora took it with her." *Stupid, stupid,* he berated himself.

"Took it with her where?" asked Officer Monday.

Billy shook his head. "Wherever she went," he said lamely.

"And where was that?"

"I don't know!" Billy cried out.

Meg put her arms around Billy protectively. "He's just a boy. Leave him alone."

"Ma'am, he's our only witness."

"And suspect?" asked Billy's father.

"And suspect," said Officer Monday, turning away as if he had tasted something foul. He did not want to consider an eleven-year-old kid a suspect, but he had no choice.

*　　*　　*

The older policeman took Billy's father away for questioning. Billy and Meg were placed under an informal house arrest. Officer Monday seemed embarrassed at the procedure.

"A girl's gone missing," he explained. "It's a very serious matter."

"Of course," said Meg. "We understand that. We'll do anything to help."

Officer Monday nodded. He believed wholeheartedly that everyone was innocent until proven guilty. But this looked bad. It didn't help that the Nolans had a reputation for being a bit odd. And this house! The walls were painted all different colors. Some rooms were empty, some staircases went nowhere. He shook his head. When a child went missing, accusations were like flames searching out dry grass. They would land on anyone and burn him up in an instant. The Nolans were in for a tough time. They would probably be abandoned by the community. Officer Monday knew the police would have to proceed very carefully.

He handed Meg his card. "You call me if he remembers anything. But you are not to leave the house. Not until we get this settled. Understand?"

Meg nodded.

*   *   *

The officer finally left. Over dinner Meg answered all of Billy's questions about Sanasarea. She told him everything she knew about Gatemakers and Travelers. She also told him about her Gatemaker, Asa Trout. Afterward Billy felt as if he was going to collapse. He went to bed, yet his sleep was troubled until finally he woke at midnight. The house was silent. He crept down the stairs and went out into the corn. A police cruiser was making hourly rounds, but Billy knew they'd be watching the front of the house, not the fields.

Billy went to the doorway and peered through. He saw nothing but the corn. He called Nora's name every couple of minutes. He sang songs to keep himself awake. When it was dawn he stumbled back through the fields. Meg was sitting at the kitchen table, waiting for him.

"Keeping vigil?" she asked.

"I've got to be there, in case she comes back."

Meg nodded. "I know. Come here."

Billy's eyes filled with tears, and he shook his head. He didn't deserve her comfort.

"Come here, lamb." Meg grabbed his hand and pulled him down into her lap. It had been a long time since she had held him this way. Billy broke down and wept.

When he was done crying, Meg smoothed the hair from his wet face and got up to make breakfast.

*   *   *

Ex-Police Chief Anil Avatar had been enjoying his retirement. He lived in a small cottage on the bay. He tended his espaliered pear trees. He walked to the village every morning for tea and a pumpkin muffin. He was expected nowhere. He had no obligations or responsibilities. He had been extremely content . . . until the morning Officer Monday called him.

The phone had rung and Avatar had grumbled. He hated to be disturbed.

"We've got a big one here, sir," said Officer Monday. "We could use your help."

"Don't call me sir," barked Avatar. "I'm retired."

"It's Nora Sweetkale. She's gone missing," said the young officer, getting right to it. Avatar was not a man for small talk.

Officer Monday himself had posted the parcel containing the blue book to Nora. He knew Avatar had feelings about the Sweetkale case, what with it never being resolved and all. He hoped it would be enough to draw Avatar out of retirement because Officer Monday was scared. There had never been a missing child in Waitsfield.

"What do you mean she's gone missing? Did she get in a fight with her mother?" Although Avatar was shaken, he didn't show it. The book! He never should have sent it. He should have trusted his instincts. The book had to have something to do with the girl's disappearance.

"Well, I . . . I don't know, sir," stammered Monday. "I haven't asked."

"That's the first thing you ask the parent of a missing kid," snapped Avatar, annoyed at Monday's incompetence.

"Satchel and Meg Nolan are involved, sir. The focus of the investigation has been on them. She was last seen with the Nolan boy."

Avatar chewed on that for a moment.

"That's no good, is it?" he remarked. An eccentric family like the Nolans was ripe for scapegoating. Waitsfield itself was ripe for a witch hunt. No, this was no good at all. This was going to get complicated. "So what do you want of me?"

"Well, we thought you could talk to the Nolan mother and boy."

"Haven't you already done that?"

"We have. We're holding Satchel Nolan at the station."

"Mmm," said Avatar, thinking.

"There's something else," said Officer Monday. "The night Nora Sweetkale went missing, her brother, David, came down with some mystery illness. The kid's hospitalized, quarantined actually, until they can diagnose it."

Avatar's mind bent and warped in a familiar, pleasurable way as he tried to make bridges between the Nolan family, the blue book, and David Sweetkale's illness.

"What are his symptoms?" he asked.

"He's like a zombie," said Monday. "Like somebody sucked the life out of him."

Somehow Avatar knew Officer Monday was not exaggerating.

Chapter Thirteen

Hours passed. The girl slept. When she finally woke, she was in a dark cottage. The windows were greasy; they let in very little light. The floor was unswept, and mouse droppings were everywhere, even on her blanket. A man stirred something at the stove. He turned around when he heard her moving.

"You've woken," he said, frowning. He walked across the room, a bowl steaming in his hands. He pulled a chair up to the bed and sat down. He smelled. No, he stank.

The girl turned her face aside and tried not to gag. The soup he offered her, however, was fragrant, and the girl's stomach was growling. He must be a good cook. The broth was laced with herbs. Pieces of an unknown meat fell from the spoon as he lifted it. The girl attempted to sit up, but soon fell back down, having no strength.

"Don't struggle so, Bean," the man grunted, his voice cracking and deep. It sounded as though he hadn't used it in a hundred years. The girl looked at him wonderingly. Ahh, so *that* was her name. But how did he know it? As if reading her mind, the man pointed to what must have been her knapsack. Sure enough, her name was stitched on the pocket. She had no idea what the *L.L.* stood for. *Bean* would have to do.

*　　*　　*

There would be no questions, for there could be no answers. Asa soon found out the girl had no memory of where she was from, or of coming to Sanasarea through a doorway on Corn Island. She certainly didn't know she was a Traveler, and Asa didn't think it was his place to tell her. She'd come to it in her own time, or she wouldn't. He would not interfere.

Asa was now sure that Bean had had a run-in with the Provisioner, but for some reason she hadn't been drained of her soul, only her memories. That was odd. He had never heard of it happening, but neither had the Provisioner ever taken an older child; usually the children were under the age of seven. Regardless, she was here, and she needed help. The time would come when Asa would take her back to the doorway, but for now she had nobody but him, and he intended to protect her until she got her memory back.

That night, when Bean was in bed, Asa watched her out of the corner of his eye. She pulled the knapsack onto her lap, took a deep breath, then emptied its contents and examined the items one by one. It was clear to him that she did not recognize any of them. The last thing she picked up was an Ancora. Asa was shocked. What was she doing with an Ancora? Had she stolen it from her Gatemaker?

How Asa longed to hold the small blue book! He had never seen one up close; he had only heard the legends. Unbidden, his hand crept up to his chest to the place where Gatemakers traditionally wore their Ancoras strapped tightly to their bodies. Asa knew instinctively he should not be staring at Bean's Ancora. Stolen or not, the same etiquette applied. The Ancora was something deeply private, and the bond between it and its bearer was sacred.

To be parted from one's Ancora was akin to having one's lungs ripped out. It meant death. That was why it was so shocking for Asa to see Bean pull one out of her knapsack. Bean's possession of it meant some Gatemaker was without one. Asa shuddered to think of that Gatemaker's fate. He realized the Ancora couldn't belong to the redheaded boy. He wasn't a robust child by any means, but whenever Asa glimpsed him through the window he appeared in good health.

The name *Ancora* came from the word *anchor*, for the book kept its Gatemaker anchored to the truth. The moment a Gatemaker was born, his or her Ancora began to write itself. There was no hiding from it. The Ancora saw and knew everything. It recorded all the Gatemaker's triumphs, as well as any misdeeds, failings, and weaknesses. The Ancora held all this information until the day the Gatemaker was ready to hear the truth about his or her life. For some Gatemakers this happened early, for others not until old age. But until the day they were ready for the truth, the book would appear blank.

Asa watched the girl lovingly handle the small blue book and wondered how his life might have been different if he hadn't been denied the things that were rightfully his. Somewhere in Talfassa was his Ancora, of this he was sure.

Bean held the book in her hands as though it were an animal, her long fingers petting the leather. The Ancora seemed to comfort her. She was obviously bonded to it, and Asa could tell it would cause her great pain to be separated from it. Somehow she had become a sort of surrogate Gatemaker for this Ancora. The mystery of the girl deepened.

"Time to sleep," said Asa, watching Bean rub her eyes. For a moment she looked like a small child, though Asa guessed her to be about twelve.

Bean nodded wearily.

"You can hang your knapsack there," said Asa, pointing to a row of hooks.

Bean looked across the room.

"No, thanks. I'll keep it with me," she said, tucking the Ancora under her pillow.

"Won't that be uncomfortable?"

Bean shook her head. "I sleep with it every night."

"Ah, so you remember something," said Asa gently.

Bean looked startled. "I guess I do."

"It's a start," said Asa. "Now, go to sleep. We've got plenty of work to do in the morning."

*　　*　　*

It wasn't long before Bean discovered the man's name was Asa Trout, and that she smelled as badly as he did. Asa turned his face aside when he spoke to her, trying not to show his disgust. Bean was ashamed and asked about a place to bathe.

That evening Asa heated water on his stove and poured her a bath in an old tub. He left the cabin, and she stripped out of her clothes and climbed in. After she had dried off with the only clean towel she could find, Bean rummaged through her knapsack and found what she thought was sleepwear. It was too small for her. The top pulled tightly across her chest, and the pants fell just below her knees.

Asa knocked on the door. "Done?"

"Yes, come in." Bean tucked her feet beneath her on the bed. Asa bent down and picked up the tub, the now-scummy water sloshing around, and carried it out the front door. It had to have weighed fifty pounds, but he managed it easily. He threw the water into the garden.

"There now, maybe you'll grow again," she heard him mutter as he carried the empty tub back into the cabin, hooked over one long finger.

Asa was not used to having company, Bean could tell. He had forgotten how to talk to people: He'd lost the basics of chitchat. Somewhere inside, Bean knew she had been taught these things. She didn't know where, or by whom, but she knew how to be polite and carry on her part of a conversation. She perked up a bit. This was something.

Asa began filling the tub again, pumping water from the large kitchen sink into a bucket, pouring the bucketfuls into the tub. He didn't heat it for himself as he had for Bean. She slid her feet into her shoes and left the cottage, closing the door behind her. She walked on shaky legs down to the shore so that he could have his bath in peace.

Bean found a little cubbyhole to crawl into, a place where two rocks made a sort of den. What a predicament she was in! She couldn't remember anything of her past, though surely she had one; she was no baby. At least she knew her name. Someone had had the sense to label her knapsack.

She also had deduced, based on the cautious way Asa was treating her, that she was *not* from this place, this archipelago. Sanasarea, he had told her it was called, 109 islands in all. She could see dozens of them from where she sat. They were islets, really, if you wanted to be precise about it. Tiny, cheerful pieces of earth scattered across the sea.

The shore of the island closest to Asa's was thick with raspberry bushes. Bean could see the plump fruit sagging from the branches. As the light faded, she saw a young woman step onto the beach. She had long black hair and wore a shawl around her shoulders. Bean sat up. "Hello," she called out.

The young woman flinched in surprise and put what looked like a small telescope to her eye, then scanned the shore of Trout Island. Bean knew she was being scrutinized. For five long minutes the young woman watched her through the telescope, saying nothing, issuing forth no pleasantries. Then she spun around angrily and walked into the brush, disappearing. Despairing at the young woman's coldness, Bean walked back to the cabin and went directly to bed.

When she woke the next morning, Asa was gone. Bean sat on the front stoop of the cottage for an hour waiting for him to return, her stomach growling. When it became clear he wasn't coming anytime soon, she sighed, walked back into the cottage, and surveyed her surroundings. It was disgusting. This would simply not do. But first some breakfast.

There was hardly anything in the cupboards, but Bean found some cornmeal with only a few bugs in it. She picked them out by hand, pinching them dead before flicking them out the window. With some water she fashioned a patty and fried it in the skillet. It was dry, not sweet, but palatable.

Bean located a broom, a mop, and some soap. She started by stripping the sheets from the beds. She held her nose as she completed this task. Everything in the cottage reeked. Blankets and rugs were dragged outside and beaten free of dust with the broom. She filled the tub she and Asa had used for bathing with hot water and dumped in sheets, napkins, dishtowels, and curtains. The linens soaked all morning, and later she spread them over the knee-high grass to dry.

Bean rested at lunchtime and boiled herself a potato. She clipped a few sprigs of parsley that hadn't bolted from the garden. She took a bite of the bitter parsley, a bite of the warm, soft potato.

She felt satisfied by the end of the day. The cottage was clean. She was pleased with her work and hoped Asa would appreciate it. She started dinner, burying some onions and a handful of chestnuts in the coals. She set another pan of water to boil on the stove; they would have to have potatoes again, since there was little else in the pantry.

*   *   *

When Asa stepped into the clearing, it was twilight. The smell of hot buttery nuts came drifting out the open windows of the lilac cottage. The curtains were bright blue again, no longer a dingy gray, and when Asa entered the cottage, it was filled with the sweet scent of soap. The birch floor was waxed back to its original honeyed hue. There was not a mouse dropping or errant seed any-where. Both beds were neatly made: blankets drawn, pillows plumped enticingly. On the small wooden kitchen table was a bouquet of purple and orange flowers that the girl must have found buried beneath a tangle of strawberry vines.

"You're back," Bean said, turning around.

Asa nodded, unable to speak. It had been so long since anyone had done something kind for him.

Bean studied him for a moment, her brown eyes animated and questioning, then went back to making dinner. Pots and pans clattered merrily. A small fire blazed and crackled. Asa sank into a chair.

* * *

The next morning Asa decided to go clamming. But first he had to say something. He cleared his throat. "Now then, there are some rules that must be obeyed if you are to live here. Better we get them straight now so that you won't be wandering around where you shouldn't be."

Bean sat down on her bed, prepared for a lecture.

"The shed." Asa pointed out the window. "You're not to go in there. It's private."

Bean nodded. "Okay. What else?"

Asa looked at her oddly. "Nothing else, I guess. Just the shed's off-limits."

"That's it?"

"Well, you probably shouldn't take the boat out. Folks don't know you're here yet." Asa tugged at his ear. "Folks don't know I'm here anymore," he muttered under his breath. "It's best you don't show yourself until we've thought of a story."

Bean bit her lip. She had already made her presence known to the young woman who lived on the neighboring island.

"But we don't have to think about that yet," Asa said briskly, for he could clearly see the girl's lower lip trembling. Not being skilled at sensitive matters, he left.

Asa hatched his plan as he walked down to the shore. It was only mid-August. There was plenty of food that could be harvested right here without their having to go to Camarata for supplies: cod, perch, crabs, blackberries, broccoli, leeks, and kale. There was a barrel of potatoes in the root cellar. There was a chicken roaming around the south side of the island that still laid eggs, and a cow and calf that needed only new pasture to graze in order to ensure a proper milk supply. They wouldn't have to leave Trout Island for weeks, months perhaps, assuming they had a mild fall. Once winter set in, however, he would need kerosene and coal for the stove, wicks for candles, and maple syrup for sweetening things. The thought of going to Camarata disturbed him. He and the girl tying up at the dock, surrounded by nosy gossipmongers . . . he put it out of his mind. The tide would be low for only another hour. He had a bushel of clams to gather.

*　　*　　*

Asa was knee-deep in mud when he saw Molly Berry coming toward him. She was stumbling along, the mud sucking at her bare feet, slowing her down. It was not possible to walk gracefully at low tide. Asa wiped his brow with his shirtsleeve and waited for her to approach. Molly looked angry, which worried him. Did she know he had stolen the Map? He hadn't seen her in years. Once, a lifetime ago it seemed, he had been friendly with the Berry family. He was shocked to find Molly had become a young woman.

"Who is she?" Molly called out.

Oh, no! thought Asa. He was not ready to explain the girl's presence. He didn't know how to explain it to himself, nor did he feel ready to reveal the few facts that he knew.

"I saw her on the shore. Who is she, Asa?" said Molly.

Asa shook his head, panicked. He had no idea what to say. Clearly Molly knew Bean was not Sanasarean.

"She came through the Veil," he said quickly. As soon as he said it, he knew he shouldn't have. Nobody had ever passed through the Veil except the Provisioner.

Molly's face darkened with contempt. "It would be a mistake to underestimate me. She's not from Sanasarea, and she didn't come through the Veil. That can mean only one thing. She's a Traveler, isn't she?"

Asa swore under his breath. It had taken only one minute for Molly to get to the truth. This was typical of a Rememberer. They cut through emotion and went directly to the facts. It would do no good to lie.

"Yes," he admitted. "At least I think she is." He would not tell Molly of the doorway on Corn Island. Not yet.

"And when did she get here?"

"A day and a half ago."

"The day after the barbecue?"

"Yes," said Asa.

Molly glared at him. "Where were you?" she cried. "Didn't you hear the emergency bell?"

Startled at Molly's outburst, Asa backed away.

"What . . . what emergency bell?" He remembered little of the day after the Map was destroyed; he had been so distraught.

"The Provisioner escaped. He got out of the Map. He stole my brother's soul!" Molly yelled.

Asa gasped. The fanciful tale he had constructed—that it had all worked out okay, that Sanasarea had escaped unscathed—collapsed.

"I'm sorry for your loss," Asa said softly, and Molly could tell he meant it. The man appeared deeply shaken. Somehow she found this comforting, but she would not back down about the girl. It could not be coincidence that the two events, the girl's arrival and the Provisioner's escape, occurred so closely together.

"I need to talk to her," said Molly.

"Not yet," said Asa. "She's in a fragile state."

"What do you mean?"

Asa sighed, his way clear now. He knew what he needed to say.

"She's lost her memory. I had no idea why, but now that you tell me about the Provisioner, it all makes sense," he lied. He pulled himself upright. "I think she had a run-in with the Provisioner as well. It tried to steal her soul but was capable of stealing only her memories."

Molly looked bewildered. "I've never heard of any such thing. She's an adolescent. The Provisioner doesn't attack anyone that old."

"Well, it attacked her," said Asa uncomfortably. He wanted the conversation to end.

"So she doesn't know she's a Traveler?"

"No."

"Well, are you planning on telling her?" asked Molly matter-of-factly.

Asa was stunned at how casually Molly discussed the situation. There was no trace of distaste in her voice. Perhaps things had changed. He had been away for so long. Perhaps being a Traveler or a Gatemaker in Sanasarea was no longer something to be ashamed of.

"Well, are you? She's going back to her own world sooner or later. She can't help who she is."

"You're right," said Asa. Molly had made clear the distinction between him and Bean. Nothing had changed in Sanasarea. But Bean belonged to another world, a world in which he imagined Travelers and Gatemakers were accepted. It was a world without a Veil; a world in which doorways into Talfassa could be made, the Aquisto attended, and destinies fulfilled.

Molly bit her lip, deep in thought. She had no idea how to make sense of all this. Perhaps the girl's arrival and the Provisioner's escape were not related after all.

"You can't sequester her here on Trout Island," she finally said.

"I had no intentions of that," protested Asa, even though he had.

"She's got no idea where she's from? How to get back to her world?"

Asa shook his head.

"Then she'll need to start school in the fall," said Molly. She turned to go. "I'll hold you to that. You can't make her into another recluse."

She began walking away, her shoulders slumped. She looked so bereft that against his better judgment Asa called out to her.

Molly turned around slowly. "Whatever happened to you, Asa? Where have you been all these years?"

Nobody had ever asked Asa this question. He looked down at his palms. The Kapth were covered in slimy muck.

"Why have you been hiding?" Molly asked softly.

Asa put his hands down by his sides. "I don't know anymore," he said sadly. "I started so long ago. It became a habit."

Molly nodded. She understood about habits. "You could change," she said. "You could join the world again. Perhaps the girl's come to help you do that."

Asa was grateful for her generosity, which in turn allowed him to be generous back. "When she's ready to talk, I'll come get you. I promise," he told her.

Molly nodded again. "The Map . . . ," she began.

Asa braced himself for her accusation.

"I've taken it on as my Lifework. Something's happened to you, Asa. You've paid a high price for the making of that Map. It's gone now, I know; somebody's stolen it, and it doesn't even matter because the Provisioner's broken out of it. Still, I want you to know I will search out the truth of it."

Asa's face flushed with color. He was embarrassed by her pronouncement, and confused.

"But why would you do this for me?" he asked. "You don't even know me. We're not related."

138

Molly's eyes teared up. "That's where you're wrong. We are related, all of us. We must all look out for one another."

*   *   *

The weeks passed in a blur. There was plenty of work to do, and Asa soon found that Bean was strong and able. Together they cleared the beach of debris and raked the sand free of shells and seaweed. They rebuilt the dock and patched the boat. They fell into an easy and comfortable routine. They were not unlike each other, Bean and Asa. Before long, Bean stopped worrying about not knowing where she was from. She knew plenty of things. She knew the names of everything around her: the plants, trees, and constellations, and sometimes the names of things that were nowhere to be found in Sanasarea. It was enough.

Each day was filled with meaningful work, and Trout Island was quickly tidied up, the gardens mulched and readied for winter, daffodil and tulip bulbs planted in the alder groves. They erected a new compost hut. The wood pile grew larger every day. It was a satisfying feeling, like money in the bank.

Bean could tell that Asa had not always lived alone. She knew the bed she slept in had at one time been occupied by somebody else. Whether it was a person or an animal she wasn't sure, but that being was long gone. Bean was good at sniffing things out. There was nobody on Trout Island now but Asa and herself.

Still, every evening after she had gone to bed, Asa would take down the skillet quietly, so as not to wake her, and scramble up an egg. He would slide the egg onto a plate, sprinkle it with chives and a little salt, open the door, and put the plate out on the step. Every

149

morning, before she woke, Asa would bring the plate back in. And every morning the egg was untouched.

*   *   *

One morning when Bean woke, there was a piece of cloth folded up on her blankets.

"What's this?" She yawned and sat up.

Asa was sitting at the table with his morning tea. He had been up for hours already. They had worked in the pasture until early evening the day before, putting up a fence. Now the cow and her calf would not escape.

He looked up from his book. Bean shook the cloth out. It shimmered as though it were made out of coins. It was the uniform of a seventh-grade Acrobatery apprentice. The stretchy one-piece suit fell down to the floor.

"Abundia," Asa said.

"Who's Abundia?" asked Bean, sliding gracefully out of bed, holding the suit in her hand.

"That would make you about twelve years old. Does that sound right?"

"I guess so," said Bean, looking down at her body.

"Well, twelve you are, there's no doubt about that. Abundia is never wrong. Come, put that down for now; the oatmeal's hot."

*   *   *

Abundia hadn't visited. Asa had simply realized that it wouldn't do to keep Bean hidden away on Trout Island, so he had invented a destiny for her, just as his mother had done for him. With

140

Molly's help he had gotten her a uniform from the Acrobatery. He had to let her go.

That morning, after Asa had explained to her more fully about Abundia and destiny and the twelve schools on Camarata, Bean put on the golden suit. It fit perfectly. Once she had it on, it seemed to adjust, to actually shift and suck itself onto her body. She couldn't tell where her skin ended and the suit began.

But what was more astonishing was what she could do. She bounced on her toes and bobbed in the air five feet above Asa's head. The air became gelatinous when she jumped in it. It held her up. It was as though she had the power to make the air change its chemical makeup.

Bean jumped around the island all morning, spinning, leaping, handspringing, landing lightly on the tips of her toes. Asa couldn't help himself. He laughed out loud with delight.

"It's remarkable," he cried as she spun around him, a whir of blurring gold. Bean knew she had been born to do this.

That afternoon, they heard the sound of bells coming from Camarata. "Able Fat-Tree," Asa said, frowning. "Dean of All Students. It means the school term starts tomorrow." His voice grew urgent. "I must tell you something now. I must tell you what I know."

*   *   *

Asa didn't sleep much that night. He worried that he should have told the girl the entire truth, that not only was she a Traveler, not only had her memories been stolen by the Provisioner, but that the doorway she had come through was still there on Corn Island

and she could walk through it back into her own world at any time. There were two reasons he hadn't. One had to do with protecting her, since the Provisioner was now roaming loose in her world. The second reason was far more selfish. In the weeks Bean had been with him, Asa had grown to love her. He couldn't imagine his life without her in it.

*   *   *

They left early the next morning.

"I don't want to go," Bean wailed, tears in her eyes, after she had climbed into the boat and Asa was about to push off. "Why can't I stay with you?"

Asa looked at her sternly. "Because you can't. Your place is at the Acrobatery. You must go. I don't want to hear anything more about it."

Bean gulped and swiped at her eyes. Her knapsack lay in her lap. One hand was inside clutching the blue book. Her golden suit was in there as well, along with her other belongings, most of which were still a mystery. Bean sniffled bravely and sat up straight. She didn't want to leave Asa, but she was excited to be around children her own age. Asa had told her about the Public Market, Sanasarea Hall and the Plaza, the fountain, the festivals, the bikes with five seats across—life on Camarata sounded wonderful.

Fifteen minutes later, the pier was in sight. Asa stopped rowing. "Eilon's Way," he told her and frowned.

"What's wrong?" asked Bean, craning her neck so she could see better. Eilon's Way was filled with boats that weaved and bobbed merrily. Children called out to one another. Brightly colored flags flew from the pilings. The sweet fragrance of fresh bread drifted over the water.

"Crowded," muttered Asa. "I didn't think it would be so crowded." He pulled his hat down low over his eyes.

"Hurry, Asa, hurry," said Bean, her excitement building. She felt like throwing up.

Chapter Fourteen

Before going into the Nolan house, Anil Avatar wandered around the farm. He found the soil dense and rich, the corn nearly eight feet high. In the barn everything was tidy and in its place: The tractor gleamed, tools hung on the wall, bales of hay were stacked neatly. There was no sign of neglect. He couldn't help but be awed. The Nolans' success had obviously come about through hard work, years of dedication, and something else: love of the land.

Avatar felt guilty that they were still holding Satchel Nolan in the station, but a month had passed since Nora Sweetkale had disappeared, and they were no closer to solving the case. Satchel would have to remain there until they made some headway. Protocol demanded it, and so did Waitsfield. Someone needed to be held accountable for Nora Sweetkale's disappearance, and as Avatar had expected, that blame had fallen upon the Nolan family. It didn't take long for Waitsfield to turn on the Nolans. Their farm stand had been broken into, the windows smashed, rotting vegetables and fruits strewn all over the parking lot.

Avatar walked quickly through the fields back to the house. He was disturbed. If the Nolans were responsible for Nora's disappearance, he should have already found something amiss, something that told him things were not as they appeared to be. He was impatient now to talk to Meg and Billy Nolan.

Meg and Billy had not been warned of Avatar's visit. He had wanted it that way. He didn't want them to know he was the ex-police chief, either. He would tell them he was another detective. Avatar walked around to the front of the house and rang the doorbell. Billy opened the door. He was small for his age, and Avatar knew immediately that the boy often suffered for his size. There were dark circles under his eyes, and he looked at the newcomer wearily.

"Don't worry, we haven't run off," Billy said, obviously used to these frequent check-ins.

"My name is Anil Avatar. I'm a detective. May I come in and talk to you and your mother?"

Billy shrugged and opened the door slowly, taking the opportunity to probe Avatar quickly. This was no rookie cop, he could tell. Avatar's mind was sharp, working on many different levels. He processed information rapidly, like a machine. Every moment he was making connections, establishing links. They would need to be very careful around him.

Avatar followed Billy into the kitchen. Meg sat at the table. There was a plate of dry toast on the table and two glasses of water. Nothing else. Avatar looked at the counters. There were no bowls of fruit, no unopened cereal boxes.

"Are you in need of food?" he asked.

"Who are you?" asked Meg.

"Anil Avatar."

"He's a detective," said Billy, trying to warn Meg with his hands. In doing so, he accidentally opened a window. There was a tiny sizzling, and Billy brought his hand up rapidly, closing it in an instant.

"What was that?" asked Avatar, seeing a small movement from the corner of his eyes.

"Mice," said Meg. "In the cabinets." Nothing in her manner showed surprise.

"Are you in need of groceries?" Avatar asked again.

"Why, yes," said Meg defiantly. "Are you going to let me go shopping?"

He shook his head. "I can't let you do that, but if you make a list I'll be happy to send someone to pick things up."

"That's not necessary," said Meg stubbornly. "I'm quite used to picking up my own things." She glanced at Billy. "We'll make do with what we have."

Avatar looked at Billy, who quickly wiped the eager look off his face. Clearly the boy was hungry.

"May I sit down?" asked Avatar.

"Do as you please," said Meg.

"I'll need to ask you some questions."

"Billy, go upstairs."

"No, I want the boy present."

Meg's face contorted with anger but only for a second. She quickly adjusted her features into a serene mask. She didn't have a good feeling about this man. Clearly he was of a different order than the other police officers. They've brought in the big guns, she thought.

"Have you been told about David Sweetkale?" Avatar directed his first question to Meg.

"Nora's brother?"

"Yes. You know he's in the hospital?"

The color drained from Meg's face. "No, I didn't," she said.

"He's not the only one."

Meg looked down at the table, as if she didn't want to hear what Avatar had to say. "I don't know what you mean," she said quietly.

"There are other children, too. All of them abruptly, mysteriously ill. It's as if the life has been drained out of them. David became sick the night Nora disappeared. Five others followed. They're all quarantined in the children's ward at Waitsfield Hospital."

"What do you mean, 'the life's been drained out of them'?" Meg asked, trying to appear calm.

Avatar frowned. "David's alive, but barely so. He's like a zombie. All these children are. They don't speak. They don't recognize their mothers. It's like they're in a waking coma."

Meg fought to keep her face composed. This could mean only one thing. Somehow the Provisioner had crossed through Billy's doorway into Waitsfield. But how did it get out of the Map? Meg silently cursed Asa. Oh, why didn't he communicate with her? What kind of a Gatemaker was he?

"Do you have any idea what's wrong with them?" Avatar asked.

Meg stared at Avatar angrily. "How would I have any idea? I've been locked in my house, my husband's being held at your station. Are you going to blame us for this, too?" she cried.

Billy kept silent, but he was terrified. At best, Meg was telling a half-truth. He could tell when his mother was lying. She knew exactly what had happened to the children. What Billy didn't question was Meg's indignation; he felt it, too. He didn't want to be blamed for anything else. But a horrible pit had opened in his stomach, for he knew that they were indirectly responsible.

"Where are you from?" Avatar asked Meg, zigzagging in another direction. It was a ploy he often used when interrogating suspects.

In all the other interviews (interviews they called them, not interrogations), nobody had thought to ask Meg this. She was unprepared for this line of questioning.

"What do you mean?" she asked, stalling.

"Where are you from originally? Your family? Your parents?"

Avatar looked at Billy, not Meg, when he asked this. He had already learned that the boy was not able to hide his emotions, and he would use the boy's responses to gauge his progress. Billy looked panicked. Bingo, Avatar thought.

"I'm from the West," Meg said coolly.

"What do you mean by 'West'?"

"Northern California, a small town called Arcata. Do you know it?"

"Can't say that I do," said Avatar.

"It's rural. A lot like this."

"Billy, do you see your maternal grandparents often?" asked Avatar.

"My parents are dead," Meg answered the question. "And I was an only child. I'm afraid I'm the last of the line." She shrugged apologetically.

"I see." Avatar leaned close to Billy. He darted in like a small animal. "Billy, did you ever see Nora with a small blue book?"

Billy's eyes widened in surprise, and Avatar had his answer.

"Did she show it to you?" he pressed Billy.

Billy shook his head. Frantically he tried to enter Avatar's mind again, but it didn't work. He was too flustered.

"Well, then, how did you know about it?"

"She was never without it. She carried it in her knapsack."

Avatar's voice was seductive, his questioning soft, grandfatherly. Billy had the sudden urge to tell him everything, to be taken under his protection. He looked to his mother for permission, but Avatar's body was blocking her from Billy's line of vision.

Avatar and Billy stared at each other. Avatar had a strange sensation of being opened up as he looked into the boy's pale green eyes. It was not a comfortable phenomenon. He felt stretched, pulled out of himself, in the presence of this boy and his mother. He had felt this way only once in his life. It was twelve years ago, the night the blue book had come into his possession. Avatar did not like this feeling. It required him to consider possibilities that had no basis in reality, and he didn't want to go there. He didn't want to go back to that night, to the one case in his esteemed career he had never been able to resolve. The relationship between that case and this one was unclear, but he knew they were connected somehow.

Out of the corner of his eye Avatar saw Billy look down at his palms worriedly. The boy quickly clasped his hands together.

"Everything okay, Billy?" asked Avatar.

"Fine," whispered Billy.

Avatar looked at the boy's hands, clenched tightly together as if in prayer. "Is there something wrong with your hands?"

"He's nervous," said Meg. "What do you expect? He's eleven years old."

"Is that true, Billy? Am I making you nervous?" asked Avatar. He felt bad. It was not his intention to make the boy suffer. It was, however, his job to pick at any vulnerability he saw, worry it up like a scab so that he could see what wound lived beneath.

"Yes," said Billy, softly.

"What are you afraid of?" asked Avatar gently.

Billy looked at his mother.

"Go ahead, answer him," she said.

"I'm afraid you won't believe us," Billy said. "You'll think there's something wrong with us. That we've done something very bad."

"Well, have you?" asked Avatar, knowing the moment was at hand. There was a moment like this in every interrogation, a space when the truth unfurled. Billy's eyes went frantically back and forth, tracking something unseen.

"No," he whispered. "We haven't done anything bad. Except for being ourselves."

Avatar said nothing. He let the boy's words linger; they had the unmistakable smell of authenticity about them. He was not convinced the Nolans were innocent of anything to do with Nora's disappearance, but he was certain that whatever their involvement, it was nothing malicious. Yes, Meg Nolan was defensive, but who in her position wouldn't be? Her husband was in jail, and she and her son were locked up in their house. But Avatar knew, with all the experience of thirty-eight years of police work, that these people had done nothing to harm Nora Sweetkale.

"I'm sorry to have troubled you," he said to Meg and pushed his chair back from the table.

Meg was shocked. She had prepared herself for a long interrogation.

"You're leaving?"

Avatar nodded. "Please give one of my men a shopping list. There's no reason for you to suffer more than you already have."

Meg sized Avatar up again. Perhaps she had judged him too quickly. She saw a small man in his sixties, impeccably groomed. Intelligence dwelled in his eyes, honesty resided in his face, but there was no malice, no cruelty. She understood Avatar had made some sort of decision about them, and he had done it in a matter of minutes, by listening intently to her son. He did not believe they were guilty. Meg was flooded with relief. She wanted to throw her arms around Avatar. For the first time in weeks she felt the world had not turned its back on them.

"I'm grateful to you," she said softly.

"Make that list," said Avatar. "If you need anything, if you think of anything, call me." He handed her his card.

*   *   *

As soon as Avatar left, Meg said to Billy, "Let me see your hands."

He held his hands up, his face pale, and Meg saw the Kapth on his palms. Her hand flew to her mouth, and she gasped.

"No!" Billy cried, shaking his hands in the air as if he had burned them. It felt as if the squares were burrowing into him.

"When did this happen?" asked Meg.

"It's been happening for months," moaned Billy, "but the past few weeks it's been worse. It's like they're trying to tunnel down into me. Like a worm."

"Oh, Billy," Meg cried. "You mustn't fight it. It's meant to be happening."

Billy clenched his jaw. "Another thing you forgot to tell me?" he snapped. He couldn't help it. Sometimes he felt so angry that his parents had left him to figure all this out on his own. Meg's face sank, and Billy was immediately sorry. They had only each other.

"They're called the Kapth," Meg told him. "All Gatemakers become marked with the icons when they enter puberty. I hadn't remembered it until just now, until I saw your palms. I met Asa only once, and that was the only time I saw his Kapth. I'm sorry, Billy. I just didn't remember."

The pain had subsided a bit, and Billy sat back down, examining his hands.

"The Kapth will get darker and more pronounced as the weeks go by," said Meg. "And then one day they'll be there for good."

"And what am I supposed to tell everyone?" asked Billy. "That you let me get my palms tattooed?"

"That would work."

"Or we could hide it," Billy suggested.

"We will *not* hide it," said Meg fiercely. "I saw what that did to Asa. By the time I met him, he was practically dead from pretending to be something he was not."

"Do you hate him?" asked Billy. He knew Meg was angry at Asa. Every day she tried to open her mind to her Gatemaker, but there was never any answer, never any sign Asa was on the receiving end.

Meg had told Billy that Gatemakers had the ability to listen in on people's thoughts. With people other than their Travelers a Gatemaker's telepathy was somewhat unreliable. Gatemakers tended to hear snippets of conversations, nothing that really made sense. Mostly this was a bother, like constantly having a radio playing in the background, and so Gatemakers trained themselves to turn this hearing off. What happened between Gatemakers and their Travelers was a much more potent and precise science. A Gatemaker could enter into his or her Traveler's mind and carry on a conversation. It didn't matter if either was in the other's presence or not. But Meg had never had that experience. Asa had never contacted her; once she had crossed over into Waitsfield, he had simply abandoned her. Billy knew Meg was crushed by this lack of contact, and now that everything had blown up, she was angry as well. She needed Asa's help.

"I don't hate him," said Meg. "I only wish I understood what happened. Do you want to try to listen for Nora?"

Billy shook his head. He couldn't bear failing again. He wasn't able to hear Nora at all. From the moment he woke up on that morning after she went through the doorway, his connection to her had vanished. Billy and Meg didn't allow themselves to think the worst: that perhaps Billy couldn't hear her because she was dead.

"What's happened to David?" he asked, suddenly remembering what Avatar had told them. "You know, don't you?"

Meg pressed her hands to her face and groaned. "I didn't think it was possible," she said. "I didn't even think. I just assumed the Provisioner was still trapped in the Map."

"Trapped?" asked Billy, remembering the first window he had made with Nora, the two of them seeing that terrifying face in the Map.

"We saw it!" he cried. "Nora and me, the first window I made, we saw the Map."

Meg placed her hand on Billy's arm. "Yes, I'm sure you did. Shall I tell you the story of the night I met Asa? The night Asa brought the Map That Breathed to life?"

"Yes," Billy said softly. "You've got to tell me everything now. Everything."

And so Meg did. But it was too late.

*   *   *

Five-year-old Tommy Pierce never saw the Provisioner coming. He was in his room digging through a bureau drawer, looking for a plastic gun his best friend Eloise had given him that he had hidden away so that his mother wouldn't see it. Music was booming from his older brother's room. Tommy hummed to himself as he pawed through underwear and socks.

If he could have talked afterward, he might have spoken about the smell of leather, the rustling of furs, the enormous shadow rising up in front of him.

He might have spoken about how he almost threw up from the thick piece of metal that was crammed in his mouth, or what it felt like to have his soul plucked from him like a banana from its peel.

But he couldn't speak afterward; he could only lie there until his mother came up to tell him it was time for his bath and found him senseless on the floor.

Chapter Fifteen

*A*sa had thought they'd left early enough to avoid any traffic on Eilon's Way, but it was the first day of school, and everybody had had the same thought; it was wall-to-wall boats.

The children were either gabbing and screaming out to their friends or morose and silent, quaking with fear. Young parents looked solemn as they sent their children off for the first time. Four-year-olds clutched their mothers' skirts in one hand and proof of their destiny, whatever sign Abundia had left for them, in the other. Parents of seventh- and eighth-graders looked positively gleeful, ready to go back to the peace and quiet of their island homes without children underfoot, squabbling and asking to take the boat out to visit their friends. Winter work would start in earnest that very afternoon.

Asa pulled his hat down low over his eyes. He had not seen these people in years. They probably thought he was dead. He prepared himself for a barrage of questions, but they never came.

Sanasareans were a strange sort. At times when you most needed things like discretion, privacy, a little breathing room, they were remarkably good at granting it. Nothing more than waves and greetings were showered upon Asa, and by the time he found an empty berth at the dock and tied up, his heart was beating wildly, as was Bean's. Neither of them had realized how much they had missed feeling as though they were part of a community.

"What's her name?" asked Marcy Willow, not unkindly, a basket of quivering eels in her arms.

"This is Bean," Asa said, carrying a basket of his own filled with quahogs he had harvested.

"And I hear she's a Traveler, eh?" Marcy said. "Come to us from a different world?" She leaned down and chucked Bean under the chin, peering at her closely as if she were an oddity. "Don't worry, child, your memories will return and then you'll find your way home."

Marcy straightened and stood up. "Poor Roane Berry. They've got him holed up in the Healery. His sister's trying desperately to find a remedy. Foolish girl. There is no cure for what ails the boy." She looked at Bean again. "Count your blessings, girl," she said, and walked off down the dock.

Asa sighed, relieved that the truth about Bean had already filtered through Sanasarea. It was just as well. It would save him the explanation. He ushered her down the pier.

*　　*　　*

The Public Market was mobbed. Stalls that were normally used for selling produce and providing services to the regular citizens of Sanasarea were transformed into booths for school supplies. Clerks yelled out their wares.

"Welcome back, Colory apprentices! Are you yellow, orange, green, blue, red, or purple this term? Don't worry, we sell toothpaste of every hue!"

"Healery tenth-graders—slings and apothecary aprons sold here."

"Cookery students—don't forget you can never go wrong with a pinch of saffron and a good whisk. We also sell burn-free spray. Make perfect golden muffins; never torch a marshmallow again."

"Gossiperians, get your Eavesdropping Aids here. Guaranteed for distances of up to one mile away."

Asa traded his quahogs to buy Bean the basics: some muscle loosener, ties to hold her hair back, soap, textbooks, and something special that neither of them could resist—a full term's supply of rock candy.

After they had gotten Bean's supplies, they went to Sanasarea Plaza to register for school. It was just as crowded here as it had been at the Market. Asa found the correct queue. The Acrobatery line was not hard to spot: All the apprentices were fidgeting, if not outright tumbling and flying through the air.

The line moved slowly; it was a long one. Acrobaterians were late sleepers, usually exhausted from darting around from place to place during the course of the day. They also had huge appetites, and most children in the line were munching on something. The Acrobatery kitchens were in constant motion. Cooks worked all through the night. In between meals there were always buckets of pizza sticks and stacks of chocolate leather on the dining-room tables.

Bean had already struck up a conversation with another seventh-grader, Peta Flounder. They were chatting amiably, and every minute or so Peta would pirouette or throw herself upside down and walk on her hands. Bean's eyes were glistening; she clutched her knapsack to her chest. She was going to have no problem fitting in, Asa could already tell. He watched as other Acrobaterians eyed Bean shyly. She was a bit of a celebrity. The fact that she was a Traveler was not held against her in Sanasarea, since it was assumed she would eventually find her way home. Because of this, Sanasareans were not threatened by her, only fascinated.

After Bean had registered, Asa told her to follow him. He had the sudden need to visit Roane Berry, to see what suffering his unwillingness to face the truth had brought about. The Healery was in a big stone building. The halls echoed, and the smell of rubbing alcohol and disinfectant filled the air. Small clusters of students whispered quietly at their lockers. A group of girls looked up as Asa and Bean passed. They were covered with red dots, a telltale sign of their second-grade status. They got chicken pox the first term, mumps the second. The second grade was commonly referred to as the year of dots and bumps.

Asa was filled with gratitude as he saw them. Being called to the Healery was a serious matter. The students had to be willing to experience every disease, every sickness and illness. How else would they be able to have compassion for their patients, or to know how they needed to be treated? It wasn't so bad as it sounded, however. Healery apprentices experienced discomfort, but they were born with something special, a certain immunity. The diseases never killed them, and they experienced pain in a softer, more distant manner, as though from another country. In that way, their education was bearable. Still, Asa thought it was an amazing sacrifice. Especially when he saw those small girls covered in red dots.

Asa led Bean through the infirmary (which was empty, it being the beginning of the school year) into a large, pleasant playroom. The floor was painted with giant flowers. The shelves were stocked with games and paints. There was a drink dispenser built into the wall. Three streams of liquid burbled out: bright green, yellow, and red.

"Lime, pineapple, and licorice cracklie," Asa whispered to Bean.

"Soda," Bean translated, a word from her past popping into her head. She shivered. It felt as though somebody were running fingernails up her back.

It wasn't until then that they noticed the young boy. He was the solitary occupant of the room, sitting in a corner. His back was rigid. His neck looked tiny, a thin, frail stem. He was gorgeous: a head of black curly hair, lips a deep dark red. Which made it even sadder, somehow, that nothing lived behind his eyes. He did not see his visitors. He did not hear them. He stared at a point on the wall, his mouth slack.

"This is what happens to most children when they meet up with the Provisioner," a voice said from the doorway.

Asa and Bean turned around. Molly walked into the room. Bean recognized the young woman who had stared at her through the telescope. She felt nervous, unsure of how the woman would treat her, but Molly paid no attention to Bean. Her eyes were only on her brother.

Molly pulled up a chair and sat next to Roane. She talked to him about ordinary things. The weather. What she would bring him for lunch. What was blooming in the garden. What fruits were ripe. The boy remained perfectly still, his eyes vacant.

"We brought him here a week ago," explained Molly. "We thought it best to have him surrounded by people, not isolated out on the island with my father and me. He seems better here than he was at home. At home, he wouldn't even sit up. Here, at least, he sits by the window. We visit every day. Children come by in the mornings and after school. At least he's not completely missing out. I have to believe he hears it somehow."

Molly stroked Roane's cheek softly. "There is one good thing that's come out of all this," she said sadly.

"What's that?" asked Asa.

"The Provisioner seems to have vanished. Dallan says she has no sense of him here in Sanasarea. At least the rest of the children are safe. For now anyway."

Asa throbbed with guilt. "So, have you made any progress?" he asked.

Molly shook her head. "The artifacts and books will reveal nothing to me. But I won't stop searching until they do," she said vehemently.

She looked at Bean as if noticing her for the first time. "Do you remember anything yet?" she asked.

"No," said Bean.

"You must keep trying. You have a home, a proper home somewhere. People who love you, who are searching for you. You mustn't forget them."

Molly's insistence scared Bean. She didn't want to be reminded of her other life. She wanted to remain with Asa. Still, she knew Molly was right.

Asa and Bean left the room quietly. They looked back at Molly, who was sitting on the floor in front of Roane, holding the boy's hands in her own. She was patting them awkwardly.

"I don't understand," said Bean as they walked out of the Healery, passing once more the group of second-graders who were now sharing a tube of Itch-No-More gel. "Why didn't that happen to me?" She was shaken by the sight of Roane. She understood now the gravity of the situation.

"I suspect it's because you're older," Asa told her. "Your soul is firmly planted in your body. It's not so with the younger children. That's why the Provisioner attacks them."

"But why did it go for me at all, then? It doesn't make sense."

"No, it doesn't," said Asa. "I've got no good explanation for you."

* * *

When Asa climbed into the boat that evening to row home to Trout Island, he was very sad. The day had gone better than he had expected. Bean was accepted readily, and more surprisingly, so was he. They had been brought back into the fold. It was clear Bean would flourish at the Acrobatery. She was a child born to be around lots of people. Not a recluse like he was.

But seeing what had happened to Roane . . . he was deeply disturbed. He had known the Provisioner was on the verge of escaping from the Map, and he hadn't told anyone. What had he been thinking? Because of him Sanasarea had been completely unprepared and Roane was dying. Asa had to do something to help.

Chapter Sixteen

It was late September. Nearly two months had passed since Nora had disappeared, and the Nolans had become outcasts. Satchel Nolan was still in custody, and other than their weekly visits from Anil Avatar (who came bearing groceries whether they liked it or not), Meg and Billy were completely isolated.

They tried to make the best of their confinement. They structured their days. Mornings they worked in the vegetable garden, weeding and watering. After lunch Meg tutored Billy. Avatar had approved his returning to school, but Meg and Billy decided it was best for him to remain at home. Meg didn't feel it was safe for Billy to go out. His only escape from the house occurred once darkness fell. Every night he went into the cornfields and waited by the door.

One night Billy heard a noise. It seemed to be coming from the doorway, from Sanasarea.

"Nora!" he yelled, peering through the doorway.

Nothing happened. The sound came again. Now he could tell

it was someplace in front of him, in the field, not from the doorway. The corn was being moved aside—trampled was more like it. Something was coming toward him. Billy began backing up as the sound grew louder. The corn parted and he froze.

It was Tria, the ruby doublecat, and she was larger than Billy had ever imagined. She stared at him for a moment, yellow eyes flashing, fur gleaming, then she sat down and began to groom her enormous paws, delicately pulling out twigs and pebbles, smoothing down the fur on her forelegs with her tongue. As Billy watched with wonder, he realized she was striped. That's what gave her fur such depth. She was actually many shades of red, perhaps *every* shade of red, but you didn't know it until you saw her up close. She rippled like a pond.

Billy extended his hand. He couldn't help himself; he wanted to touch that astonishing fur. The Kapth glinted on the palms of his hands. He drew his arm back and examined the squares. They had gotten darker just as Meg had said they would; they were now a deep blue. For the first time it didn't feel strange to have the Kapth; it almost seemed natural. He extended his hand to Tria, and she licked his fingers. She let Billy stroke her. She may have even purred before she ran off into the night.

The next evening Billy was back in the corn well before midnight. He couldn't wait to see Tria again.

"Where's Nora, girl?" Billy asked. "Do you know? Is she all right?"

The doublecat stared past him into the corn.

Billy tried again. "Well, if you won't tell me where Nora is, will you tell me why you've come?"

163

Tria sighed as if utterly bored and rolled over on her back, her powerful legs unfolding. The fur on her belly was the color of strawberry Life Savers. Billy felt ridiculous. What was he thinking, talking to a cat, even if she had come through the doorway and was the size of a pony? He lay back in the corn and began picking out constellations. He nibbled on some stale Goobers he found in his sweatshirt pocket and waited for Tria to make the next move. But he hadn't expected anything like this: She wanted him to climb up on her back.

"Oh, n-no you don't." Billy was afraid of heights.

Tria nudged him with her gigantic head, and then bit him on the ankle.

"Ow!" Billy yelled. She bit him again, on the wrist.

"Not fair!" he screeched, jumping into the air.

Next thing he knew, he was sitting on Tria's back and she was purring contentedly. He nursed his sore wrist.

"That hurt, you know," he told her. "You didn't have to bite me."

Of course Tria didn't respond; she simply began moving. It was not a smooth ride. The doublecat lumbered back and forth trying to find her balance. Billy could tell she was not used to carrying anyone. But she was powerful—he could feel her muscles move beneath him.

"Where are we going?" he asked, clutching two tufts of fur in his hands.

Tria turned abruptly to the right. Her nose twitched rapidly, her eyes scanned the trees, and she took off with a bound. Billy almost fell off.

"Hey, not so fast," he cried, trying to regain his balance.

Tria stood perfectly still, and he righted himself. He had one second to catch his breath before the ruby doublecat took off again at full speed.

It was the most amazing ride he had ever had. Flight was more like it; he and Tria flew through the night. Billy had never been athletic. He had always been a bookworm. "More cerebral than most" was the way his father put it. Still, sometimes he thought he would have traded all his brains to be able to run without tripping, to hit a softball and make it to first base, to swing hand to hand from the monkey bars. That night on Tria's back, for the first time in his life, he was an athlete. With the doublecat beneath him, he was graceful and sleek. The two of them were indistinguishable from each other. Sometimes Billy couldn't tell where Tria ended and he began, and he knew this was precisely the point.

Tria flew through his father's woods, up the irrigation ditches, along Lily Creek, through the corn, down the corridor of elms to the Little Swamp. Billy nestled into her back. He quickly found out that the best way to ride her was hunkered down and low; that way everything flew with them, was them. It was the most glorious thing Billy had ever experienced.

That night Tria left the Nolans' land. She took Billy first down Curtis Corner Road, past the charred remains of their farm stand. It had been burned down a week ago. A halfhearted effort was made to catch whoever did it, but the investigation was dropped pretty quickly. Billy knew why: People thought the Nolans deserved to have their livelihood destroyed; they were finally getting their due.

"Hurry up, girl." Billy urged Tria on past the farm stand. He couldn't bear to see it.

She took him into town, where they roamed the deserted streets. Nobody was about. A curfew had taken care of that. The children of Waitsfield were under siege: Ten children had been attacked by the Provisioner and were quarantined in Waitsfield Hospital.

Tria sauntered down Main Street with Billy on her back. They went past Kenyon's Department Store, past the tiny record shop called Fat Albert's, past Woolworth's and D'Angelo's. They took a left at Old Mountain Field and the doublecat became a blur, running around and around the basketball court in wild circles. Billy didn't fall off once. I'm a Gatemaker, he kept whispering to himself. *A Gatemaker.* Tonight that felt like a magical thing. His willingness to stop hiding his true nature was the glue that kept him stuck to Tria's back.

Through the small town she carried him; over the guild bridge, through the gardens of the stone library, then down past the university. The boy and the giant cat were nothing but a red streak. It was only when Tria took a left onto Ministerial Road that Billy felt something was wrong. Ministerial Road was lined with rhododendrons, which made it feel like a tunnel. There were no streetlights. Tria slowed down to a trot, and a sour smell assaulted Billy's nose.

"Gross!" he shouted, pinching his nostrils shut. He heard the rustling of furs, the clinking of metal. He whipped his head around, searching frantically in the dark woods on either side of him.

"Did you hear that?" he asked Tria, but she seemed to hear nothing. She kept padding down Ministerial Road. Billy pitched forward on Tria's back. He cried out as all sense of balance left him. Hang on, he thought. He knew he was still sitting on Tria's back, but then again, he wasn't. Some part of himself had come loose and was drifting out into the woods, untethered.

Billy was terrified and thrilled at the same time. His senses were heightened. His nose was like a wolf's and could translate layers of scent: dirt, decaying leaves, wild onions, a dead mouse.

Then he saw the Provisioner hiding behind a tree. He and Tria came upon the Provisioner quickly, as if carried on a wave. Billy flailed and kicked, he tried to backpedal. He knew what was required, and he didn't want to do it. But he had no choice. In the last moments before his consciousness descended down into the Provisioner's, Billy saw a small yellow house, a child's bedroom window, and then he was inside the Provisioner's head looking out at the next victim, five-year-old Eloise Markham.

Eloise stood in her room making a circle of dolls around her bed. "This is a magic circle," she said.

"Why magic?" asked her mother.

"For protection."

"Protection against what, honey?"

"Against whatever got Tommy," she said.

"Oh, El," her mother crooned. "You have nothing to worry about. That's why we're keeping you at home, until we know the bad germs aren't out there any longer. And haven't we been having fun, making Popsicles and Play-Doh and the fort under the table?"

Eloise shook her head. Her eyes filled with tears.

"What is it, El? Tell Mom."

"I miss Tommy."

"I know, honey; so do I. But you'll see him soon, I promise. As soon as he comes out of the hospital. In the meantime, can we put those dolls away? I'll trip on them in the middle of the night."

Her mother picked the dolls up and put them in the toy box. "There, isn't that better, sweetie?"

Once her mother was gone, Eloise climbed out of bed. She opened her toy box and took out her dolls. She dragged her blanket into the middle of the room, and one by one she laid the dolls in a circle around it.

"This is a magic circle," she said. "Nobody can cross it unless I say so. I am under protect—"

Her words were cut off as a leather bridle slid over her head, a metal bit crammed into her mouth.

The Provisioner groaned as the girl's soul began wafting into the air. It thrust the bit more fully into her small mouth, and the soul emerged. It was a lacy, thready thing, for the girl was young.

Billy watched in horror, helpless to stop it. He felt everything the Provisioner felt. It was blind with hunger, and at the core of the Provisioner was a deep inner coldness, a coldness of the sort that could not be penetrated. Emotion surged through the Provisioner, and Billy was driven deeper, deeper. The Provisioner's memories pierced Billy like lightning bolts, sword thrusts, each hurling him into another spasm of pain. A decrepit apartment building. A giant of a man named Rip. An abandoned fairgrounds. Then there was rage—such brittle, all-encompassing rage that Billy thought he would suffocate.

He tried to claw his way out from behind the Provisioner's eyes. This was a mistake. The Provisioner felt Billy's presence like a thousand bees in its head. The Provisioner roared, knelt, and began to bang its head mercilessly against the wooden floor. Billy's mind felt as though it would *shatter. Through blurred eyes he saw Eloise Markham's unnaturally still body on the floor, and he began to scream.*

*   *   *

When Billy came to, he was lying in the road. Tria stood over him, a paw on either side of his body; she was guarding him. Billy moaned and rolled over onto his hands and knees. He spit and retched, trying to get the taste and smell of the Provisioner out of his mouth. Never had he connected with another so deeply. He hadn't carried on a conversation with the Provisioner; he had been in him, *become* him. Billy stared at the Kapth. He felt contaminated from what he had just experienced, but he also felt thrilled. He had done what he was supposed to do. He was fulfilling his destiny.

Suddenly Billy jumped up. The fairgrounds—he had been there! Zendalet Fairgrounds. His father had taken him there when he was little. It was closed down now, had been for years.

"Let's go, Tria," he said, straddling the giant cat's back.

The night was not over yet.

Chapter Seventeen

Bean adored school. She was more agile and graceful than practically anyone except Peta, who was her equal in most things and better than Bean at the ground arts: spinning on her toes, doing splits, standing with her leg against a tree. Bean excelled at aerial feats. She was not afraid of heights, and leaping was second nature. She and Peta flew around Camarata in their golden suits, appearing out of nowhere with a glide and a *whoosh*.

Seventh grade was a turning-point year at the Acrobatery. Bean and Peta watched the upper-level students and began to understand the subtleties of what was ahead of them. It was their job to stand at the edge in seventh grade, to be the fastest, the quickest, to be a blur. But soon they would be striving for something beyond doing daring, breathtaking acts.

Seniors were the complete opposite of seventh-graders. Seventh-graders never stopped moving, whereas seniors seemed to expend no energy; their goal was the conservation of movement. They hovered fifteen feet in the air. They wore shimmering blue suits, iridescent as bugs' backs. Most of the time it was hard to tell they were even there. Whole tribes of them would simply hang in the air. Every minute or so they would shift, adjust their limbs, change position. They were indistinguishable from the sky.

This was where Peta and Bean would find themselves at the end of their apprenticeship at the Acrobatery. But in seventh grade their purpose, what would give them the highest marks, was to be dazzling and brave and bold. And so they were.

Asa climbed into his boat every Friday afternoon and arrived in Camarata in time to have dinner with Bean. It was their weekly ritual. He rented a room at Uda Cricket's boardinghouse. Uda was a gracious hostess, and there was always a plate of raisin cookies ready for him.

"I don't know how you do it. All that pasta," Uda would say to him when he returned from the Acrobatery dining room. Her hands would rest on her wide hips, hair coiled up in two buns on the sides of her head.

"Nothing but starch those children eat, sugar and candy. Tell me, did you have spaghetti?"

She'd lean into his face and cackle, knowing full well he had had spaghetti. That was pretty much all they served at the Acrobatery.

"Here, then, have your port."

She'd hand him the crystal decanter, and sometimes she would even join him, and it was not altogether unpleasant. She would catch him up on the gossip. She always fell asleep early and in midsentence, her large head collapsing on her chest. Asa would cover her with the tablecloth, as there was never a blanket handy, and then he'd climb the stairs to his room.

On Saturday mornings Asa went to the market for his weekly groceries. He stocked up on bread, wax, soap, truffles, and his one splurge—a volume of poetry from the bookseller.

*   *   *

Once a week, the twelve schools on Camarata would open, and there would be readings, performances, feasts, concerts, case studies, and lectures. All week long, students were required to stay at their schools, but on Saturday afternoons and evenings they could attend whatever school they wanted.

It was usually clear what school you were from. All the Acrobatery apprentices wore skintight, seamless suits. The Healery apprentices could be distinguished by their limps, sallow skin, crutches, and the collapsible vessels they carried around in their pockets to whip out for sudden onsets of nausea. Students from the Beautery walked around admiring everything. This was the least exciting school to Bean. It seemed like a subject she might be more interested in when she got older. *Maybe.* These children did seem older than their years.

The Gossipery students spoke in whispers and hisses and carried on conversations under the stairs. Bean never felt safe around them. But Peta also described to her in detail the positive benefits of gossip: how there were times when information needed to be spread, and how skilled the Gossipery apprentices were in disseminating it in just the right manner.

The students from the Cookery were usually a mess, their

172

faces smudged with flour, the tips of their fingers burned, their hair smelling like chicken potpie or onions. But Bean liked them; they tended to be good-natured, and they were generous. They always had snacks for the Acrobatery students, who were always hungry.

The Colory students, however, were the most fascinating to Bean. Each grade was a different color, for how else would you know how to use color unless you *became* that color? The students began changing color in July or August and by September, when school began, they were fully changed. All the first-graders were green, second-graders red, third-graders blue, fourth yellow, and so on. Everything about them turned the color they were inhabiting: their teeth, their hair, their skin, even their eyes.

Once Peta and Bean had been doing zooming sprints out in the back meadow, which was carpeted with asters. The girls zoomed low over the purple flowers. They swam through the air, their feet barely touching the ground. They did this for a long time, until Bean realized that several sets of eyes were staring up at her, blinking slowly. Then the field sat up. It was filled with sixth-grade Colory students, who were such a vibrant and believable shade of purple they had been indistinguishable from the flowers they were pretending to be. Bean was so astounded that she lost her balance and fell on top of them. There was lots of umphing, "I'm sorry"ing, and "didn't know you were there"s.

Oh, it was marvelous to be on Camarata with all the other children. Bean was so busy, she barely thought of her predicament. But at night, when she crept into bed exhausted, her legs trembling from the day's activities, she wondered if there was somebody out there looking for her, somebody worried, somebody who loved her besides Asa. She lifted up her pillow and touched the cover of her blue book. She always slept on top of it; it consoled her, made her feel less lonely. She rifled through the pages time and time again. They were always blank. She had thought about beginning a journal of her own in those pages, but she couldn't bring herself to put one mark upon them. Even though they were bare, they felt rife with importance. She would put the book on her covers, sigh deeply, and fall asleep in seconds.

*　　*　　*

One afternoon Bean was sitting in class when she heard a scratching sound coming from her knapsack. She knew it was the blue book, which occasionally rustled around. She was used to that, but this scratching was different, louder and more insistent.

She raised her hand. "May I be excused?"

The teacher, Miss Ballymone, looked at her dourly. Bean was not her favorite; Miss Ballymone did not see why a Traveler was allowed to attend the Acrobatery. She had formally protested Bean's arrival but had been overridden by the rest of the board, who were more than willing to take in the girl who had faced the Provisioner and survived.

"What now?"

"The bathroom," said Bean, hating Miss Ballymone for embarrassing her.

"Very well." The teacher waved her away.

Bean slung her knapsack over her shoulder and got up.

"Leave that here."

"I won't," said Bean, her temper rising. The scratching noise was getting louder, more frantic. She had to get out of the classroom.

"You insubordinate brat!" cried Miss Ballymone. Her voice grew snide. "You're lucky we even allow you to attend the Acrobatery."

Bean was silent, stung with shame. Her cheeks burned as if she had been slapped. She ran out of the classroom and down the corridor.

When she got to the bathroom she locked the door. She sank down to the floor, her chest heaving, out of breath. That stupid, mean woman! But the teacher was right: She didn't belong here. What was it Molly Berry had told her? That she had a home, a proper home somewhere. People who loved her, who were searching for her. But what about Asa? Didn't she belong with him now? She felt so confused, so torn. Molly's words reverberated through her. *You mustn't forget them.*

The book! Bean had almost forgotten about it in her humiliation. The scratching noise had stopped. Her knapsack was perfectly still. She undid the clasp and drew the book out carefully, inhaling deeply. Seeing it was like breathing air, receiving oxygen. They were deeply loyal to each other, she and the book. Bean stroked the cover lovingly and opened it. The white pages were no longer completely blank. There, on the first leaf, was an inscription.

If you are reading this, the time of revelation is near. You who could not bear to look upon the truth until now. The day is almost at hand. Let there be no judgment. Let the information you read pass over you and through you like a gentle rain, no matter how painful, no matter how hard. And at the end, when you are through, let there be stillness. Let there be under-standing. And may you finally know peace.

Bean burst into tears. She wasn't sure why she was crying. All of a sudden she felt exhausted, as though she had been waiting her entire life for these words to appear, for some guidance to come, some direction. And now, finally, it had, and she had no idea what it meant.

Bean sat in the bathroom for an hour. She couldn't bear to go back to class. At last she crept down the hallway and left the Acrobatery; she had a desperate need to see Roane, to be in the presence of somebody who asked nothing of her.

This was not unusual, Bean visiting Roane. Every day after dinner she went to spend time with him. She had been told there was very little hope he would recover. The Provisioner's victims were able to live on for only a few months in their vegetative state. She couldn't bear to think of Roane dying. She believed he could hear even though he wasn't able to talk.

When Bean walked into his room at the Healery, Roane was alone, and she was grateful. She ran up to the boy and threw her arms around him. He was drooling a little bit, and she wiped the spit from his face with her sleeve. She was not disgusted. There was some faint memory of having done this before, having loved a little boy so much that she was not disgusted by anything he did. Bean felt very small. She did not feel twelve. She buried her face in Roane's curls.

"What's happened?" someone asked gently.

Bean lifted her head. Molly stood in the doorway of the room.

"Nothing, he's the same," said Bean sadly. "No change."

"I wasn't talking about him," said Molly, walking over to her. "What's happened to *you*, Bean?"

The concern in Molly's voice made Bean burst into tears again. Molly put her hand on the girl's back and let her weep. When she had cried herself out at last, she peered up at Molly's kind face. The young woman looked smart and capable. She looked as though she could be trusted. Bean took the blue book out of her knapsack and held it up to show her.

Molly looked stunned. "Why, Bean, whatever are you doing with an Ancora?"

"You've seen one of these before?" Bean was shocked.

Molly stuck out her hand, and Bean gave it to her. Molly turned the blue book over and examined it. Bean fought to hide her discomfort but was not successful. She cried out as a terrible pain went shooting down her arms.

"Here!" Molly thrust the book back into her hands.

As soon as the Ancora was back in her possession, the pain subsided. Molly looked at her wonderingly. "Well, you continue to be a mystery," she said. "Do you know what that is?"

Bean shook her head.

"You shouldn't have it," said Molly, frowning.

Bean stared at her in horror. Had she made a mistake in showing Molly her book? Was she going to try to take it away?

Molly saw the fear in Bean's eyes. "I won't take it from you," she said. "That's not what I meant. Clearly you are bonded. It would cause you great harm to be separated from the Ancora now, but I suspect you know that, don't you?"

Bean nodded.

"What I meant was that an Ancora is not for a Traveler. It's for a Gatemaker. It's unusual that you have it. No, it's beyond unusual, it's . . ." Molly struggled to find the right word. "Extraordinary." She was choosing her words very carefully. Bean was skittish. Clearly something had just happened to shake her up.

"Do you come to visit Roane often?" Molly asked, changing the subject, hoping it would calm her down.

"Every day," said Bean softly, clutching the Ancora.

Molly did not like the hold the Ancora had on the girl. This was not right. This was abnormal, and it worried her greatly.

"That's good," she said. "I'm sure he loves your company." She looked at her brother, his lifeless face, his slack body. "I'm going to save him. He's going to recover," she said fiercely.

Bean nodded. She didn't doubt it. Molly seemed capable of anything.

"Has Asa seen your Ancora?" Molly asked.

"Yes," said Bean.

"And he didn't tell you what it was?" Molly was amazed. "He didn't say anything?"

"No."

Molly shook her head with frustration and sighed deeply. She didn't want to be the one to give Bean the information, but Asa had left her no choice.

"It's a book traditionally given to Gatemakers when they come into their power at adolescence. The book is the accounting of their life. The Ancora is a log of everything they have done, things they are proud of, things they would rather forget. It remains blank until the day they are ready to hear the truth about their lives."

"So it couldn't be about me?" asked Bean. "It couldn't be the accounting of my life that's in the book?"

"I'm afraid not," said Molly. "It's somebody else's Ancora you've got there. Chances are, that Gatemaker is no longer living."

Bean looked dismayed.

"You are going to have to remember on your own, Bean. It's not going to be given to you. You have to *want* to remember. You have to want to go back to your home. Understand?" Molly spoke firmly. She could see the effect her tone had on the girl, who seemed to crumple with disappointment and fear.

"Are you mad at me?" whispered Bean.

"No, Bean, I'm not mad." She looked at the girl closely, studying her tear-stained face. Why, she's just a child, Molly thought, and she found herself filled with empathy for Bean's plight.

"I'm not mad, just concerned," she said. "But let me worry about that, okay? You need to go back to the Acrobatery. You'll have been missed by now."

"Okay," said Bean, turning to go. She spun around in the doorway. "I am trying, you know. To remember."

"I know you are," said Molly. "You may be with us a long time. You may be with us just a little bit longer."

Bean shuddered. Both options were equally frightening. She was no longer sure what she wanted.

"Go back to the Acrobatery," instructed Molly. "It's where you belong for now."

Bean nodded, grateful to have some direction.

*   *   *

Asa had a peaceful day on Trout Island, as all of his days had been lately. He had not gone back to his old ways after Bean had started school. He had something to live for now, and he took pride in his home. He'd given the cottage a fresh coat of paint, and it glowed a luminous lilac that pleased him. He missed Bean desperately, but knew that he had done the right thing by insisting she go to school.

And the Map, something was happening again to the Map. Asa wouldn't have believed it possible, but slowly the Map was regenerating itself. The torn pieces of canvas that months ago had hung raggedly from the frame had stitched themselves together. The white translucence was reappearing. Sometimes Asa could even detect movement, something glimmering below the Map's surface. Occasionally bluish spidery lines like veins surged across the canvas. It was not *his* Map that was returning, not *his* Talfassa, for that was gone, but the Map as it had been before he had touched it, before he had brought it to life.

One evening, moments after he had locked the shed (he spent time with the Map every day, as if visiting an ill relative), Molly Berry strode into the clearing.

"She's got an Ancora, Asa!" she yelled.

"Hello, Molly Berry," said Asa, bracing himself for another interrogation.

"An Ancora! What's she doing with an Ancora?" Molly asked him, her hands on her hips.

"I don't know," he said.

Molly glared at him. "You know she's bonded with it? If it's taken from her, she will probably die?"

"I know that," Asa said softly. He decided the best way to deal with Molly was to agree with her. This seemed to temper her anger.

"But it's not hers!" shouted Molly in frustration. "Doesn't that worry you?"

Asa sighed. "It's a mess," he admitted. "But what are we to do?" He frowned. "If only her memory would return."

Molly was not convinced Asa was telling her the whole truth. "It's more important than ever that you encourage her to get her memory back," she said. "She's in danger."

This seemed to reach Asa; he looked very troubled. Molly knew he loved Bean and would never want to see her hurt, never mind be the one responsible for inflicting the pain. Molly studied him as emotions flicked across his face. Asa had changed since Bean's arrival. He looked healthy and happy, he had gained some weight, and Molly knew Bean was responsible for that. She was glad for him. He had his whole life ahead of him.

"I'm still working on the Map," she offered, softening.

Asa nodded.

"I think I may have a theory."

"What's that?"

"It hasn't all come together yet. But it's something about Talfassa, the Talfassa depicted in your Map."

Asa did not like the turn this conversation was taking. "What about it?" he asked slowly.

"Why was it a Map of Talfassa?" Molly countered.

Asa shrugged, trying to appear indifferent. "Why not?"

"No," insisted Molly. "There's got to be a reason." She looked deeply into his eyes, and Asa frantically looked away. It was not a pleasant experience to be scrutinized by a Rememberer. "Asa, why do you long for Talfassa so? Why do you yearn for something that's so clearly out of reach?"

Asa kept his hands pressed down against his sides. He had not been hiding the Kapth when he was alone on Trout Island. Not using the camouflage paste had freed him. He felt like a child, his innocence restored. He knew the Kapth were glowing in response to Molly's question. Asa made a decision, fast, so he couldn't change his mind. He lifted his hands, exposing his palms to her. The Kapth sizzled and blue sparks spat into the air. Molly did not blink.

"So you *are* a Gatemaker!" she cried.

Although Molly hadn't gotten anywhere close to translating the scroll that came along with the Map, she had given much thought to the Map and to the idyllic Talfassa that it portrayed. It looked too perfect to her; she knew no place was that perfect, unless it was in somebody's dreams. Involuntary tears streamed down Molly's face. She was as surprised as Asa at her sudden display of emotion. She swiped her cheeks with the backs of her hands.

"Why are you crying?" asked Asa. "I'm the one who's lived a life of lies. You should despise me."

"I don't despise you. You lied because you had no other choice. Because you weren't allowed to be yourself," said Molly. "It's just . . . it's just so sad. Nobody should have to live that way. It's an injustice."

"Would you stay for supper?" Asa asked suddenly, handing her his handkerchief.

"Supper?" Molly wiped her nose and eyes. She had never been invited anywhere for supper. She always took her meals at the Remembery.

"Yes, supper," said Asa. "I've made oyster stew. There's far too much for one person to eat."

Now Molly felt like running. What in the world would she think of to say? A dinner conversation; she had never had one. She shifted her weight nervously from one foot to the other. But she wanted to stay. She wanted to hear about what it was like to be a Gatemaker. She wanted to see Asa make a window. But mostly she wanted to be part of this world, the world where people ate together, laughed together, worked together.

"Yes," she said.

Chapter Eighteen

"I think we may have made a mistake," Billy whispered.

He and Tria stood in front of the gate to the fairgrounds. The sign that had once stretched between the two giant posts had partly fallen off and was hanging precariously by a chain. It creaked eerily as it swung in the breeze. Billy tilted his head sideways to read it.

HEAVENLY ENTERPRISES WELCOMES YOU TO ZENDALET FAIRGROUNDS! The heads of a pair of blond children bobbed cheerily on the dark metal, their pudgy hands holding cones of cotton candy and pinwheel lollipops. Billy shivered. The sign gave him the creeps. It was from another time: The children seemed doll-like, not like real kids.

He was scared. "I think we better go," he said, but Tria side-stepped around the giant sign and carried him forward onto the fairgrounds.

Billy crouched low on her back and looked around. All the old rides were still there—the red-and-white-striped Ferris wheel, the spinning teacups, the merry-go-round—but the rides were off-center, tilted, and skewed. The metal was rusted. Seats were torn out of the roller coaster. The horses and chariots were scarred with graffiti. He shuddered. It was like being in a graveyard.

Tria stopped.

"What is it, girl?" asked Billy.

The doublecat sank down on her belly. Billy didn't want to get down—he felt safer on her back—but he knew she must be tired, so he slid off. They were surrounded by small wooden shacks, the old concession stands. CORN DOGS, POPCORN, SALT WATER TAFFY, read the signs. Billy's mouth watered.

"What do you want?" a small voice said.

Billy jumped and spun around. A child, maybe five years old, was watching him from behind the counter of a clam-cake shack. It was a towheaded boy. He looked exactly like the one on the sign, only this boy wore clothing two sizes too big for him. He surveyed Billy with a gaze that was far too mature for his age.

"What do you want?" the boy repeated.

"I'm not sure," said Billy.

"Why are you here?" the boy asked.

"Because I'm looking for something," said Billy. He walked toward the boy slowly. "Perhaps you can help me."

"Why should I help you?"

Billy changed tactics. "What are you doing out here alone? It's not safe. There's a curfew. Don't you know that?"

The boy shrugged and ducked out of sight.

Billy groaned. "Now what am I supposed to do?" he asked

Tria. She looked unconcerned. She laid her head on her paws as if she were ready to go to sleep.

Billy turned toward the clam-cake shack hesitantly. He needed to go find the boy, but it was the last thing he wanted to do. As he was walking toward the shack it began to glow with a soft orange light. Then all the old concession stands filled with the same soft light, and behind the counters people appeared with candles in their hands. There were men and women, some of them stooped and elderly, others middle-aged. There were more children, babies, toddlers, and a small group of teenagers. Within seconds Billy was surrounded. The people of the fairgrounds stared at him. Some of the children came out from behind the counters and made a circle around Tria. They gazed at the double-cat with wonder. Tria let them climb on top of her. She let them bury their faces in her crimson fur. The children shrieked with delight, and the adults watched silently. Finally an old woman spoke.

"Who are you?" she asked.

"Billy Nolan," Billy answered, pulling himself up to his full height. He had the sense that this woman was the leader of this tribe. He probed her but found he could hear nothing. He did not know if it was because she was empty or because he was drained after the run-in with the Provisioner.

"Your dad Satchel Nolan?" the old woman asked, her face contorting into a mass of wrinkles.

"He is," said Billy cautiously.

"He's a hard worker," she said approvingly. "A steward of the land."

Billy had never heard his father referred to as a steward before, but he liked the sound of it, the respect that it implied.

"We are stewards of this fairgrounds."

"I can see that," said Billy. He liked the way this old woman was talking to him. As if he were an adult. As if he should be taken seriously.

"You live here?" he asked.

"We do. We don't bother anybody, and they don't bother us," she told him, making it clear she wanted to keep it that way.

Billy nodded.

"What is it that you want?" the old woman asked, staring at Tria.

"Rip," said Billy. "I'm looking for a man named Rip."

"I don't know him," the old woman said. "Carol Rose," she yelled to a red-haired woman in the shack next to hers, "you know anybody named Rip?"

"No," Carol Rose answered, but she asked the man in the booth next to hers. "You know a guy called Rip?"

And on this went until all the people who lived in each of the concession stands had been asked and answered in the negative. Billy tried hard to listen in on their thoughts, to see if they were telling the truth, but their minds were scattered and far away. He strained, but could hear nothing.

"Well, there you have it," said the old woman. She looked up at the sky. "I'd say you better be getting home now. Your dad'll be worried about you."

Billy felt weak with disappointment. Had he been wrong? Had he misheard or misinterpreted the Provisioner's memories? It was a dead end, he realized dismally. Rip could be anyone or anywhere. His Gatemaking powers had not served him well; they had misled him.

"Thank you for your time," Billy said sadly. "I'm sorry to have bothered you."

"Don't remember us to anyone," warned the old woman.

Billy shook his head. "I won't." Defeated, he climbed on Tria's back and was carried out of the fairgrounds and into the woods again.

"The Nolan boy, was it?" asked Rip, emerging out of the shadows of the Ferris wheel.

Nobody was used to the sound of his voice yet. It was gravelly and deep, and it startled the old woman.

"We were protecting you," she said.

"You did right, Alma," said Rip, shrugging into a battered barn jacket. "But it's time for me to go."

"It's not safe out there," said Carol Rose, drawing the blond boy close. "You know that. Something's out there."

"I know," said Rip. "That's why I've got to go."

The man named Rip followed Billy home. He kept a safe distance so that the boy and the giant cat wouldn't know they were being tracked. Rip could tell by the slump of the boy's shoulders how forlorn he was, how sad. He was an outsider, this boy. Rip knew, for he was an outsider, too.

The cat dropped Billy off in the backyard, and Rip watched him climb the back steps wearily and enter the house. He felt sorry for Billy. The boy had gotten a bum deal; everyone had lied to him. Rip watched the house until the sun began to rise, and then he walked quickly to the Nolans' barn and climbed into the loft.

Chapter Nineteen

Bean was out of sorts. She had lost her rhythm. She kept stumbling. She had accumulated injuries: a stubbed toe, a bruised knee, and a good-sized lump on the back of her head.

"Just what are you doing?" asked Miss Ballymone snootily. "Are you practicing *any* of your skills?"

"Of course I am," said Bean. It wasn't for lack of practice that all grace seemed to have abandoned her. It was because she was distracted; all she could think of was the Ancora.

Bean wanted to understand it. If the Ancora belonged to a Gatemaker, why did she, a Traveler, have it? Did the Ancora belong to *her* Gatemaker? And why wasn't her Gatemaker in touch with her? Was he—or she—dead? And if he was, how would Bean ever find her way home? Her questions were endless.

That night she couldn't sleep. The Acrobatery dormitory was quiet. All the girls were bundled up in their beds. Some of them were moving their limbs; students in the accelerated program did calisthenics even in their sleep.

When she got out of bed, Bean did not put on her school uniform; instead, she slipped into her regular clothes: pants, wool sweater, and green boots. She slung her knapsack over her shoulder and crept down the stairs. The Acrobatery door shut softly behind her. She looked up and saw that the lights were on in the sophomore classroom. It was a well-known fact that some muscles were more active at night than in the daytime. Sophomores worked out all night long in order to stimulate those muscles. Bean could see them floating above their desks in their butter-colored suits.

She walked down to the dock. She looked longingly across the bay; she missed Asa desperately. She could see a small lantern shining through the trees on Trout Island. It was a sign; Asa was awake, too.

*   *   *

Asa had not been able to sleep. He could not get Molly's words out of his head. He knew she was right, that things were much more serious than he wanted to believe: Bean *was* in danger; she was abnormally attached to the Ancora. It was vital that she go back to her world and try to solve the mystery. He couldn't keep her here in Sanasarea. As much as Asa had grown to love her, as much as he wanted to protect her from the Provisioner, he *had* to bring her to the doorway on Corn Island: It was the right thing to do.

He sat at the table, nursing his cup of tea, and thought back on his dinner with Molly. The lilac cottage still felt alive with their laughter and talk. Asa was amazed that his confession had not sent Molly running. Instead, he had found that by revealing he was a Gatemaker he had set himself free. Molly had stayed long into the night, and they had not run out of things to say. It had been a surprise for both of them, the pleasurable evening. Asa looked around the cottage with contentment. Bean's arrival had changed everything. He knew he would not go back to being a recluse even after she was gone. His dinner with Molly had assured him of this, for he had discovered he was not a recluse by nature, only by circumstance and habit.

Asa slammed his hand down on the table with conviction. He would not hide the Kapth again, on or off Trout Island. Sanasarea would have to accept him. He would not pretend to be something other than what he was.

The Kapth crackled and glowed as if in response to his decision. Asa lifted his hands from the table and examined his palms. The Kapth were something to behold, symbols of his power, the truth of himself, and in realizing this a dead part of him slid away. In that very moment a voice popped into his head. It was as clear as bells, as if somebody had materialized in the lilac cottage. *Help us, Asa! Help us!*

Asa stared at the Kapth in a stupor. He knew that voice, though he hadn't heard it in years. It was Meg.

*   *   *

"Asa?"

Bean stood in the doorway of the lilac cottage. Asa was sitting at the kitchen table staring into space. His eyes were heavy and glazed. He appeared to be listening to something.

"Asa, are you asleep?"

He turned slowly and looked at Bean as though she were a stranger. "Does it look like I'm asleep?" he asked softly.

The room was dark except for the faint glow of the fire. Asa stared at Bean for an uncomfortably long minute, then got up and rummaged around in the ice cabinet. He pulled out an apple cake, sliced off a piece, and slid it onto a plate.

"Eat," he told her.

Bean obediently sat down and picked up her fork. Asa sipped his tea, and Bean ate the cake. She caught the last of the crumbs with her fingers.

"I haven't been honest with you," Asa said.

"You didn't tell me what the blue book was, that it was an Ancora," said Bean, swallowing uncomfortably. "I know. Molly Berry told me."

Asa frowned. "My list of transgressions grows longer. But it's something else I'm talking about. Come, I must show you," he said.

He rowed them to Corn Island in silence. They did not speak to each other. Bean felt sure her time in Sanasarea was almost over. The sense of Sanasarea as home had vanished, and she was groundless. But the groundlessness did not feel scary, it felt right. The two of them dragged the boat up on the shore.

"Follow me," said Asa, and he led Bean through the cornfields into the very center of the island to the doorway.

Bean gasped. She knew without Asa telling her that through that doorway was her real home. She knew because every cell told her so. In that instant her memories came flowing back to her.

A red-haired boy named Billy popped into her head. "Want one?" he asked, grinning, holding out a pretzel. Then she heard his voice, calling her. "Nora, Noraaaa, where are you?"

She began to cry, big gulpy cries, and with each sob a piece of her past came back to her. She was on a roller coaster with her old life speeding up in front of her: her brother David, the monkey bars at Waitsfield Elementary, Big Macs, Del's lemonade and strip pizza from Caserta's on Federal Hill, seeing *The Sting* at the Campus Theater, Meg and Billy and the doorway on the island of corn. And her mother. She cried out. Oh, how she missed her mother!

Asa watched Bean as memories descended upon her. She smiled, she laughed, she wept, and she yearned. And when it was over, when she had incorporated her past back into her body and stood in front of him limp and exhausted, Asa said proudly, "Well done, Bean." He was amazed at her strength and her courage.

She looked up at him. "My name's not Bean, it's Nora," she said gently. She didn't want to hurt him. He had known her only as Bean. He had given her that name, she realized.

"Ahh," said Asa, feeling the sharp pang of loss, trying to make sense of the girl standing in front of him, his Bean and somebody else's Nora.

"What do you mean, 'well done'?"

"You understand why you got your memories back?" Asa asked.

"No," she said.

"Because you're ready to hear the truth."

"What truth?" asked Nora hesitantly, wondering if her readiness had anything to do with the Ancora beginning to reveal itself to her.

"My truth, to start with, and soon after that, I suspect, yours. But first there's something on the palms of my hands you must see."

Asa then told Nora of his life. He started at the very beginning, with his mother inventing his destiny sign. He told Nora about Talfassa, about the Aquisto—the school for Travelers and Gatemakers—and about the night he made the Map and his Traveler went through a doorway. He confessed to Nora that he had stolen the Map and soon after that, right before Nora had arrived, the Provisioner had escaped. Finally he told her about Meg contacting him that evening, and he relayed everything that was happening in Waitsfield: the children in the hospital, the Provisioner on the loose, the search for Nora, the Nolans' suspected involvement.

"Billy's mother is your Traveler?" asked Nora. "Meg?"

Asa nodded.

"It's too much!" she said, feeling dizzy.

"Give yourself a minute," said Asa. "But you must take it in. The Provisioner is roaming free in your world. The Nolans are in trouble, and worst of all, children are dying." He gestured to the doorway. "You must go."

Nora panicked. "But I'm not ready to go!" she said. "Please don't make me leave."

Asa looked startled. "But your home is there, one step through that doorway. Don't you understand? Don't you want to go?"

"Not yet!" Nora cried. "I've made a second home with you, don't you see? I can't just leave it without saying good-bye. I've got to collect my things. Please, Asa, it will only take an hour. Take me back to the lilac cottage once more!"

She was so distraught. What damage would one more hour do? Asa thought. Besides, he wanted to have a proper good-bye as well.

"All right," he agreed.

*　　*　　*

At the same moment that Asa and Nora climbed into their boat to row back to Trout Island, Molly Berry was readying her own boat. It was dark out, she could barely see; morning wouldn't arrive for another four hours. Molly wasn't taking much: a sandwich, an apple, a blanket, and a picture of Roane. She was scared. She knew there was a good chance she would never return.

"I know what you're doing, Molly Berry," a stern voice called out.

Molly looked up and saw Dallan walking briskly toward her. She was shocked. Dallan hadn't left the grounds of the Remembery for nearly fifty years. Seeing her mentor on the docks of Camarata was all wrong.

"What are you doing here?" Molly whispered.

Dallan peered down at her, looking like an ancient girl in her nightgown, her long hair loose around her shoulders. "You'll need more than an apple and a blanket to make it through the Veil," she said.

Molly frowned. The old Rememberer knew everything. "I'm going. Don't try to stop me."

"Very well," said Dallan. "But you won't make it through. And even if you did, the answer is not to be found in Talfassa."

"But what else am I to do?" Molly cried. "I've got to do something. The artifacts are telling me nothing. The books are closed to me. There's got to be a way to bring Roane back!"

"Perhaps the answer is not in the books or artifacts. Have you considered that?"

"But it's got to be somewhere," Molly insisted.

"It is," Dallan agreed. "It's in your heart, my girl. Your gentle, generous heart."

Molly began to cry. "So what do I do now?" she sobbed, looking up at the old woman who stood silent and protective beside her. "How do I help him?"

"It's not complicated," said Dallan gently. "You are not required to go through the Veil or catalog any artifact or book or put your life at stake. All you have to do is love him."

Part Three

Chapter Twenty

Nora walked through the doorway of the cottage timidly, as if she were a stranger seeing it for the first time. This saddened Asa, but he tried not to show it. Everything had changed. In a few hours she would be gone. Nora plunked down wearily into a kitchen chair. She pulled the Ancora out of her knapsack and placed it on the table. She laid her head down upon the book; the coolness of the leather was comforting.

"I'm so tired," she said in a little voice. "Perhaps I could take a nap."

She did look exhausted, but Asa knew he had to get her moving. He could not let her dawdle. What was ahead of her was grim. He didn't know what the outcome would be, but he did know she had to deal with the mess she'd left behind in Waitsfield.

"No nap. You must open your mind to Billy now," Asa said firmly. "I'm sure he's been trying to contact you."

Nora sighed, lifting her head from the table. "How?"

"Empty your mind. Make a space for him to enter," he instructed.

She frowned. "But how do I do that?"

"Think of nothing."

Nora nodded. She focused and tried to think of nothing. She screwed up her forehead and stared intently at the wall. Then she started thinking about the licorice whips at the Nolans' farm stand and wondering which children in Waitsfield had been attacked and if Billy was still mad at her for pushing him out of the way.

"This will not do," said Asa.

"But what if Billy doesn't want to talk to me? What if he hates me?" Nora said miserably. "I betrayed him. I think I gave him a concussion."

"He may well hate you. You did betray him." Asa was cool. "You were sneaky, and you stole the opportunity to go through the doorway instead of asking for it. However, it was the correct instinct. You are the Traveler, not Billy."

"I hope he'll forgive me."

"You'll have to ask him for that," he said gently. "Now focus. You must let your mind loose. You must be in a receiving place, then Billy will be able to find you. The collaboration between you two is your strength; it's your weapon."

Asa left Nora, scowling away with her efforts, in the kitchen and walked out to the dock. What went on between a Gatemaker and a Traveler was private. He did not want to overhear their conversation.

*　　*　　*

Back in Waitsfield, Billy was searching for Nora. It was not an easy task. He, too, had to focus. He, too, had to loosen his mind, but at the same time he had to tighten it. He tapped on the seams between the two worlds of Greenwater and Waitsfield. Some places were softer than others, and he could feel Nora's presence more strongly. In these places he would insist. There was no better way to describe the process than that—he simply insisted on her presence and finally, after many tries, he found her.

"Billy, are you there?"

"I'm here. It's me," he said. His voice was calm. He sounded quite unlike himself. Billy felt a quiet power pulsing in him as he made the connection with Nora, and he tried to direct this calmness to her. She needed it; he could hear the panic in her voice.

"Oh, God," Nora moaned, doubled over with guilt. "Do you hate me?"

"No, I don't hate you."

"But I was greedy and selfish. I thought only of myself. I pushed you out of the way. Will you ever forgive me?" she said.

"Yes, I forgive you. You were the one meant to go through, not me. If I had gone through, who knows what would have happened? Things would probably be a lot worse here, and they're pretty bad as it is, let me tell you."

"Oh, Billy, I'm so sorry. Asa told me what's happened to your family. I never thought that would happen. I never thought I would lose my memory. I planned to come right back; you've got to believe me!"

"I do believe you," he said. "But you didn't come right back. You've been gone for months. My father is in jail. Our farm stand was burned down. The Provisioner came through the doorway. And eleven children are about to die."

Billy did not tell Nora these things to make her suffer, only to make sure she knew exactly what was at stake. He purposely did not tell her David was one of those children. He needed Nora to keep her wits about her. He needed her to be strong.

"What do I do?" she asked.

Good, thought Billy. He could sense that she was pushing her exhaustion aside. "You need to get back here. Now." His voice was urgent. "I don't think we've got much time."

"I'm coming. Asa's going to take me back to the doorway on the island of corn," she said. "I should be home in . . ." Nora's voice began to fade.

"Nora, speak louder; I can't hear you."

"The Ancora. There's this . . ."

Billy groaned. A cacophony filled his head. He covered his ears. It sounded like a crowd, like thousands of people talking at once. He desperately tried to pick Nora's voice out.

"It's doing something. Can you hear it? Can you hear the scribbling? It hurts, Billy, oh, God, it . . ."

"Nora!" Billy yelled.

But she was gone.

*   *   *

At that exact moment Rip woke in the Nolans' barn. Something was about to happen. He felt a prickling sensation, a growing unease, as if whatever had been gestating was now about to be born. This was the moment he had been waiting for.

He slid open the barn door and slipped through, careful to make no sound. He looked at the Nolans' house. The lights in the kitchen flicked on, and he saw Billy Nolan walk briskly through the room, fling open the back door, and gallop down the stairs. Billy cupped his hands and bellowed out, "Tria. Triaaaaa!"

Rip knew the boy was calling the ruby cat. He called many times, but Tria did not come. Finally, clearly disappointed but unable to wait any longer, Billy began running toward the fields.

Rip began running, too.

Chapter Twenty-one

*T*he blue leather cover of the Ancora flew open with great force. It slapped the wood of the table violently, and the table shuddered as if it had been hurt. Nora stood and took a few steps backward. She did not know what was happening, but it seemed best to stand clear. Pain ribboned through her, and she took deep breaths, trying to absorb it. She knew instinctively that the best way to deal with the pain was to surrender to it, not to fight.

The pages of the Ancora began to rustle, as if somebody were blowing on them very softly. They made the sound of a bird moving about in its nest, the sound of soft feathers on twigs. The pages began to turn, slowly at first, then faster and faster. Soon the Ancora was a blur of fantastic motion, and Nora felt as though she was being spun, too, her insides tossed and turned. Dizzy, she closed her eyes, grabbed the chair, and held on. A scribbling sound filled the room. Her eyes flew open. She saw words, sentences, dancing in the air in front of her. She could make no sense of them. It was an old-fashioned cursive writing that was hard to read. The words flashed before her, then plunged down into the Ancora, disappearing below the surface of the pages.

This went on for what seemed like hours, though really it was only a few minutes. Nora thought she would pass out, but she didn't. She managed to hang on. She knew it was her job to tolerate it, to bear witness to what was happening. When it was done, when the Ancora stopped moving, she felt weak, as though she had been trapped in the bowels of a ship for months and months and finally was able to stagger above deck into the sun.

Nora picked up the Ancora. It was no longer completely blank. A page in the middle of the book was filled, and she began to read it as she had been destined to do.

February 8

"She looks normal," Lucy Trilling cried out. "She's not an aberration. You're wrong! She's beautiful. Nora, we must name her Nora. It was my mother's name. She shall have it, too."

Lucy's hand searched for paper and pen on the bedside table. Exhausted, she gave up. "You do it, Armadon. I have no more strength. You must write down our daughter's name."

Lucy lay in a pool of blood on a dirty mattress in a tenement building in Waitsfield. She had labored for twenty-two hours to have this baby. She had done it without help of any kind. She had been sick from the first moment of conception. Nine months into the pregnancy she was bedridden and barely recognizable, her features swollen unnaturally, her skin a greenish blue. The man named Armadon, the father of the newly born child, had refused to bring Lucy to the hospital or to get her medical attention of any sort. She had never been seen by a doctor. The baby's growth had never been monitored, and by suppertime that evening, Lucy would be dead.

Armadon betrayed no emotion. He did as Lucy requested. He wrote the child's name on a pad of paper, underlined it as if for emphasis, and placed the pad on the bedside table. He sat beside her silently, and pretended for the last few hours of Lucy Trilling's life that she had a future. And when it was done, when Lucy had finally died, he stayed in his chair, unmoved even by the sounds of his own child's screams. He made no move at all until there came a pounding at the door. A loud voice demanded that he open up. Then he moved; quickly, efficiently, violently, his arms rising up like weapons, the Kapth on the palms of his hands gleaming a steely blue. He left the baby and the dead woman behind.

Nora looked up from the Ancora, stunned. February 8. *Her birthday.*

She had just read the story of her birth. Her mother was a woman named Lucy Trilling. Her parents hadn't died in an airplane crash after all! She had always suspected there was more to her story, and for a moment the bitter taste of triumph flooded into her mouth, but it was short-lived. Her father was a monster. A Gatemaker, but a monster nonetheless. He had refused to get help for her mother; he had let her mother die. And he had left her. Nora began to cry. It was far worse than she'd ever imagined. She *was* an orphan after all, only she had been abandoned, left voluntarily, and her only legacy was her cruel father's Ancora.

Nora threw the book across the room in a rage, then cried out in agony at being separated from it. Her vision clouded. Her body felt leaden, and then predictably, the pain began. It shot from her toes up the length of her body. Groaning, she stumbled across the room and bent down to retrieve the Ancora. She clasped it to her chest, and the pain slowly subsided.

Oh, why had she ever started on this journey? Why hadn't she left things as they were? Why had she thought there was something better than the life she had?

*   *   *

Nora burst out of the cottage, weeping. Asa spun around on the dock. What could Billy have said to put her in such a state? She ran into his arms, undone.

"I hate him! I hate him!" she screamed, unable to get her father's emotionless, stony face out of her mind.

"Hold on, hold on," said Asa. "What's wrong?" He knew this wasn't about Billy. Something else had happened.

Nora shook her head wildly. She couldn't bear to speak of it. She felt deeply ashamed and wanted only to forget what she had read. Then she remembered her mother's words. *You can't sit around waiting for a father to appear. Maybe someday you will get a father. Maybe you won't. And maybe you'll have to choose one yourself.*

"I choose you," Nora sobbed into Asa's chest, hoping that, if she said it out loud, it would become true. "I choose you."

"Oh, brave girl," said Asa, smoothing her hair back from her face. "My precious, brave girl. I choose you as well. Now tell me what's happened."

*　　*　　*

Molly walked down to the Deeps with a platter of cod in her hands. The smell of the fish was pungent, even though it was salted and dried, and she'd been breathing through her mouth ever since she had left the Remembery's kitchen. The lovelies were sprawled on the cool floor of the Deeps in a tangled pile of brightly colored legs. They smelled the cod before Molly walked through the doorway and ran to greet her.

"Okay, okay," she said, laughing as the lovelies nuzzled her legs and butted against her. They looked like walking carpets, she thought. Plush, bright fabric. Molly walked into the Deeps and placed the platter on the table, which was strewn with books and artifacts, all of them uncataloged, all still a mystery. The double-cats jumped up on the table and began eating. Molly was amazed at how evenly they portioned out the fish.

After they were done with their meal, they congregated around Molly, who sat at the table. She had not been to the Deeps in days. She had been spending all her time with Roane. She did not miss it, she thought, looking around her at the alcoves stretching up clear to the ceiling. She remembered when she had first come and Dallan had turned on the almandine lights. Oh, the ambition that had flowed through her! The anticipation, the longing to make a name for herself! She sighed. That ambition was gone. In its place was something softer, more patient. She could wait. She had other things to attend to. She did not know how much longer Roane would live, but she did know how her brother would spend the rest of his days, with her by his side.

The green doublecat, the mother, twined herself around Molly's legs. "You are a sweet one," Molly said, bending down and petting her between the ears. The doublecat twitched her nose agreeably and began to purr. Molly buried her face in the bright fur. It smelled like hay.

Molly felt tired. The scroll that had come along with the Map was sitting atop a pile of books. She hadn't looked at it in a long time. Molly cleared a space on the table and carefully unrolled it. She ran her fingers lightly across the lettering on the parchment and began to hum. She let her mind drift; she sifted through a mixture of memories, smells, ideas, colors, and always she came back to the mother lovely, the softness of her fur, the gentle purring.

And then it happened. The language that had a moment ago been foreign, impenetrable, suddenly became clear. Whether the language had been translated or whether the translation was happening as she looked at the words, Molly did not know. All she knew was that she understood it. She began to read.

*   *   *

Nora let Asa read the Ancora. He was silent after he read it, and she didn't push him for a response. He looked troubled. Nora had lived with him long enough to know he needed time to digest the information.

"I have something to share with you, too," said Asa. "I'd like to show you the Map before you leave."

Nora nodded in what she hoped was a supportive manner. She didn't hold the theft against him. She understood the significance of his offer: Each was sharing a deep secret before they parted.

Asa unlocked the shed, and sunlight poured into the tiny room. "Here," he said, falling to his hands and knees. Nora sat down beside him.

The Map was propped against the wall, a blanket thrown over it. Asa flung the blanket aside, and in that instant Nora remembered seeing the Map through Billy's window that long-ago day on Moonstone Beach. She remembered the beauty of it, the intricacy of the drawing, the vibrant colors. And now she knew the name of the thing that had been imprisoned in the Map: the Provisioner. Nora shuddered, thinking of its gruesome face. She forced herself to pay attention to the matter at hand.

The Map had changed. No longer did it depict anything. It was blank, but far from dead. It looked as though it was waiting. It was nearly translucent, made from the thinnest, most pliant material. White ribbons undulated across its surface. It made her yearn—for what, she didn't know. Nora reached out, then she brought her hand back quickly, embarrassed at her urge to touch it.

"No, go ahead," said Asa. "It's okay." Perhaps she would be the one to bring the Map to life again.

Hesitantly, Nora stuck out a finger and touched the surface of the Map. It was an odd sensation, like touching very cold skin. She felt a current of power running through her and cried out. Touching the Map filled her with anticipation, as if she was about to be given what she had always wanted most. But nothing else happened. No image appeared. The Map stayed blank, and Nora pulled her hand away, disappointed.

"Oh, Asa," she said, knowing he must have been doing the same thing during the past weeks, hoping the Map would respond to him once again, give him back Talfassa. She looked up at him. His face was guilt-ridden. "You did what you thought was best, taking it."

Asa shook his head. "It was the wrong thing to do." He reached one long finger out and touched the Map sadly, then he turned the canvas back to the wall. "We've got to go." He ushered Nora out of the shed.

"You're not going to lock it?" she asked, for the shed had always been locked.

He shook his head. "No more locks."

Asa and Nora walked down to the dock.

*   *   *

Molly's arms were riddled with goose bumps. She felt light-headed with anticipation. She began to read.

This Map has ears, has eyes, it breathes
Known by many names; known not at all
It is wind and storm, mutable and wild
It is spear and knife, hungry for the mark
It is hawk and eagle; it sees far and wide
It is possibility and fate

The Map will take you where you most want to go
It will conjure the province of the heart
But, voyager, be warned
This territory is rarely what you expect
So think carefully on the difference
between dream and desire

For if you call on the Map
If you waken it from slumber
You must agree to play by its rules
Simple they are
Easy they are not
And they must never, ever be broken

You may not turn away
You may not change your mind
You may not send another in your place
If you do any of these things
You risk destroying the Map
For above all, the Map cannot bear disloyalty

So if all these warnings have not sent you running
Then stand in front of the Map and admit that you are lost
But be ready to jump, to leap, to plunge,
As a divine pact you've made, and faithful you must be
For this Map has ears, has eyes, it breathes
And it wears your most secret face

Molly looked up from the scroll, electrified. The lovelies, sensing something big was occurring, gathered close. Her guess that the Map of Talfassa was somehow linked to Asa's yearning was right. Talfassa appeared on the canvas because that was Asa's heart's desire—where *he* most wanted to go. Had somebody else stood in front of the canvas and confessed he was lost, a different Map altogether would have appeared.

But how did the Provisioner end up in the Map instead of Asa? Molly didn't think the Provisioner went in willingly. Nor did she think Asa pushed it in—he wanted more than anything to go to Talfassa. It made no sense. No, something else must have happened. There must have been some struggle; the Provisioner must have fallen into the Map accidentally. That would explain it! That's why the Map never cleared, and the image of Talfassa had remained imprinted on the canvas. The wrong person had gone into the Map, so the Map kept depicting Asa's heart's desire. Like a stuck record, skipping over and over again, only for years.

Molly stood up, alarmed. The Map was a significant and potentially dangerous artifact, one that could cause great harm. Asa had activated it unknowingly. That could happen again if it got into the wrong hands. Molly hurried out of the Deeps, the lovelies following her. She went to Dallan's room; she searched the libraries, the refectory, the dormitory, but the old woman was nowhere to be seen.

*   *   *

"So you've found your father," said Asa as he paddled them across the channel to Corn Island. "It's not such a bad thing. It's good to know the truth. Better than having it haunt you."

"I don't want him," said Nora bitterly. "I want nothing to do with him."

"I'm afraid it's too late for that. You've got his Ancora. The page that made itself known to you is in the middle of the book. That means his story has not ended. He's alive."

Asa did not look at Nora when he said this. He didn't want to worry her. But he knew that if she had her father's Ancora, surely he was looking for it and would eventually try to get it back. Nora's journey was far from over.

"Well, where is he, then? How could he not come?" she demanded. Then in a very small voice she asked, "What kind of a father would not come?"

"That I don't know," said Asa. And he didn't. He couldn't imagine not coming to Nora's aid; not protecting her, sheltering her.

The rowboat bumped against the shore of Corn Island. Asa climbed out and pulled the boat up on the rocks. He extended his hand to Nora, and they stood for a moment, looking back at Trout Island.

"I don't want to go," said Nora.

"I don't want you to go, either," said Asa. "But you must. Billy is waiting for you. Your mother is waiting."

"What will happen to you?"

"What do you mean, 'what will happen'? Nothing, of course. Life will go on as usual." Asa said this to placate Nora, but he was not sure it was true.

"You won't become a recluse again? You've got to promise me that, Asa!" It was more than she could bear to think of him retreating back into his solitary world.

"Ah, no, my girl, that won't happen," he said. "I'm back now, here in my world, where I belong. I'm going to tell the truth about myself. There will be no more hiding."

They tramped through the corn and in a few minutes stood at the doorway. Nora stared at it with wonder. It had been here the whole time. A few steps forward and she would be home. She shivered.

Asa kneeled and took her by the shoulders. "No more hiding for you, either," he said. "You've learned many things about yourself. Many truths, not all of them easy to bear, but all of them yours. You must shoulder them. You must carry them with you. Like it or not, they are yours."

Nora nodded. She was crying. "Can I come back?" she whispered.

"Of course you can come back," murmured Asa, drawing her close. He held her tightly. She was trembling.

"NO!" a scream came hurtling through the doorway. The voice was unmistakable. It was Billy's.

Nora and Asa broke apart quickly as a dark shadow loomed over them. It was the Provisioner. Because it was in the doorway between the worlds it was shrouded in a gauzy film. It didn't seem to see them, not yet. Nora jumped back, terrified, as the Provisioner's hand poked through the doorway first as if testing the temperature, the child-sized bridle dangling obscenely around its wrist like a purse.

"Oh, God," Nora moaned as she realized what she had to do. She could not let the Provisioner come back into Sanasarea. She backed up quickly and, summoning up all of her Acrobatery strength, began to run, her hands outstretched, her body like a plank. She leapt through the doorway, pushing the Provisioner back into Waitsfield, and the doorway immediately sealed up behind her.

Chapter Twenty-two

*T*he Provisioner staggered backward and fell to the ground. It appeared to deliberately fall in slow motion, almost as if it were patronizing them, and Billy watched with dread, knowing the Provisioner would soon get up with renewed vigor.

Nora did not fall so gracefully. She hit the ground hard, cried out, and lay still, her arm twisted unnaturally beneath her. Billy ran to her side.

"Get up," he pleaded, watching as the Provisioner rose to its feet. "Please, Nora, you've got to get up!"

The Provisioner rolled up to a standing position like a pill bug, its body constructed of neat sections. Billy suspected this stiffness was unnatural. He was sure that the Provisioner had had a life *before* it was the Provisioner. Where that life took place, who the Provisioner really was, this was what they needed to find out.

Nora was quite certain she had broken something. Groaning, she pushed herself upright with her good arm and saw the Provisioner watching them from across the clearing. It didn't seem to be in any hurry. Nor did it seem alarmed to see Nora getting back up.

"We don't have a chance," she moaned.

"Give me your hands," ordered Billy, kneeling on the ground next to her. He'd long ago figured out they were no match for the Provisioner's strength. They would have to overcome it in a different way.

Nora attempted to lift her left arm and shrieked. It was indeed broken. "I can't," she whimpered. "Don't ask me to!"

"You must!" shouted Billy. "It's the only way."

An overwhelming weakness enveloped Nora then; she felt she simply could not go on. Her journey had been too long. She had learned far too much about things that she didn't want to know. All she wanted to do was sleep.

"You're giving up so easily?" asked Billy softly. "Do you want to die?"

"Of course I don't want to die," she whispered feebly.

"Then find whatever strength is in you—and I *know*, Nora Sweetkale, that strength is enormous—and call it out! NOW!"

Billy's words were potent, and Nora felt them rock through her. She could not ignore his summons. She shut her eyes and, shaking wildly, lifted both her hands to meet Billy's. The pain was agonizing, sluicing through her in waves, but though she screamed she did not falter.

Just before the palms of their hands met, Nora shuddered, for the Kapth were searing hot, and she could feel the heat singeing her face.

"Once we make contact, you mustn't let go," whispered Billy.

"I'm afraid."

"I'm afraid, too."

"Will it burn me?"

"I don't think so. You're going to travel again. Only this time you're going to travel through me. I'll be the doorway. Are you ready?"

Billy swiveled his head around and looked anxiously at the Provisioner, which was still watching them from across the clearing. The Provisioner was visibly reorganizing. It seemed to be changing shape, becoming more compact and solid. Its eyes grew steely, its pupils elongated like a goat's.

"We've got to hurry," urged Billy.

"Where am I going?"

"Into the Provisioner." Billy touched the Kapth to Nora's palms.

*   *   *

It was a whole different kind of traveling, a kind that was not usually attempted without years of schooling and practice, but Nora and Billy didn't have years, they had only moments. Instinctively but blindly they blundered their way into the most intimate collaboration that could occur between a Gatemaker-and-Traveler pair.

As it turned out, the process was more painful for Billy than Nora, for it required him to prop himself open, which was excruciating. The pain of Nora's broken arm was minor in comparison and soon dulled; the Kapth served as a kind of anesthetic that allowed her to travel without physical discomfort.

As for Billy, his job was to delve deeply into the Provisioner's mind, to make his will a searchlight. He raked through its memories and thoughts and then created a current in himself that drove what he had collected out through the Kapth.

Nora's hands, and then her entire body, were surrounded by a quivering blue light dotted with silvery constellations. At first it was a wondrous thing, the light spinning around her like cotton candy. Then the light solidified, and Nora found herself in a room.

The room was empty except for a giant bunk bed, eleven beds high. She craned her head up. Each bed was neatly made, the blanket drawn over the pillow. A ladder connected the beds like a vertical trestle.

"Go ahead. It's your job to explore." She heard Billy's voice clearly in her head.

Nora looked at the bottom bed. There was nothing there.

"Pull the blanket back," Billy ordered.

She hesitated. The sheets were stretched taut.

"Pull it back."

"All right, all right." Nora pulled down the blanket and jumped back in fright. Under it was a child—or something that had once been a child. This bag of skin was flattened out as if its organs had been removed from its body. She peered into its face. She knew this girl. Eloise. She had lived a few streets over.

"Next bed." Billy was relentless, but he knew he had to be. Nora was scared; she could still turn back, and they could not afford to let that happen. She had to know what was at stake.

Nora stifled a sob. She was standing in a room that contained all the bodies of the Waitsfield children whose souls the Provisioner had stolen. Billy made her turn back all the blankets, and when she had gotten to the top bunk bed, she was nearly frantic. Her head hit the ceiling as she crouched on the ladder. "Ouch!"

"One more."

"Don't make me do it anymore!"

"You must."

In the last bed was her brother, David. He was the youngest of all the children, and he was in the worst shape, for he had been the first victim. His face was barely recognizable. Nora cried out and fell from the ladder, her arms flailing.

"Don't let go of me!" yelled Billy, for even though Nora had been traveling, she had never lost contact with Billy's hands. "Somewhere else, I'll take you somewhere else!" He sent the next vision spewing forth from the Kapth.

All of this was happening very quickly. It felt like much longer but only seconds had passed—seconds within which the Provisioner strode across the clearing. It knew it was inhabited, and it was beating its ears with its fists, trying to get Billy out. It roared with fury. The blue light encircled Nora again, and a memory materialized, falling over her like a shroud.

She was standing in a corridor where two men were crouched on their haunches staring at a door numbered 404. The men were very large; they had the same shaggy hair and the same coarse features. It wasn't until they rose and lifted their heads that Nora understood they were twins.

The sound of feet clattering up the stairway. A small, dark-skinned policeman. His gun drawn. "You call about the noise?" he asked the two men.

They looked ashamed. "Yes," said one of them. "I'm afraid we're too late."

"What's your name?" the policeman asked.

"They call me Rip."

"That your brother?"

"His name's Robbie."

The policeman nodded. He rapped on the door with the butt of his gun.

There was no answer.

"Open up," he bellowed, then he burst open the door.

Though nobody could see her, Nora moved a safe distance away from the men. She felt sick. She knew what was about to happen. A baby wailed. Nora knelt and began to retch. "Get me out," she moaned to Billy. He did not answer her.

There were two gunshots, then a ripping sound, and a doorway appeared in the hallway. Nora looked up despite herself. Even after all he had done, she still found herself desperate to see her father. Would there be any love in Armadon's eyes when he looked at her?

"That's your father?" Billy was shocked.

Nora moaned, unable to answer him, too intent on watching what was happening. Her father didn't see her, since she was really not there, only a bystander in this memory. He plunged through the doorway, and one of the men followed him.

"Rob, don't go!" Rip roared. But it was too late, the doorway sealed up behind them.

In a rage, the Provisioner wrenched Nora and Billy apart, scattering the particles of its memory everywhere. A blue ash rained down on them. The Provisioner yanked Nora up by the neck and began to wring her throat. Billy collapsed on the ground. The energy it had taken to make himself a doorway had been enormous. He panted frantically, unable for the moment to come to Nora's aid. His limbs simply wouldn't move.

Nora fought desperately, despite her broken arm. She swung both feet forward, slamming them into the Provisioner's chest.

The Provisioner grunted and stumbled backward, and Nora slid from its grip.

She ran back to Billy and gave him her hands. "Again. Send me again," she demanded.

"Look for things," Billy gasped. "You won't be seen. I know only what the memory knows, but you can learn more. Do you understand? You can travel into the memory and walk around in it."

Nora nodded, and Billy pressed his palms to hers.

She was in a library. Or what used to be a library, for this library had no books. The shelves were bare.

"I have something for you, Robbie. A gift. For helping me to recover."

Nora's father brought out a small velvet box. "This was given to me by my father, and now I give it to you." He opened the box. Nestled in the silk was a thick braid of indigo-colored metal about a foot long.

"What is it?" asked Robbie.

"Pick it up and find out," Armadon said with a faint smile.

Nora was feeling more courageous this time. She inspected her father carefully. He said he had recovered. From the gunshot wounds, perhaps, but clearly he was still very weak. He did not have his Ancora. She did.

Robbie shook his head. "I don't want it. I want to go back. Make another doorway."

"That's simply not possible," said Armadon. "I've told you that."

Robbie winced and squeezed his eyes shut, as if to close out reality.

Armadon sighed. "Take it, my friend. It will make your life better. I promise you."

Robbie looked at the metal braid again. "What does it do?"

"It will stop your yearning."

This was exactly the right thing to say, for it was what Robbie wanted most. He picked it up.

Instantly the braid came to life, writhing and shuddering in his hands. Horrified, Robbie threw it on the floor, and it coiled about at his feet, hissing. Then it darted at him and encircled his ankle. Once, twice, it wrapped around, cinching his flesh tightly. It had become a manacle, and Nora's father had not lied; it did indeed put an end to Robbie's yearning. It also put an end to every emotion, every single thing that had made him human. That day a Provisioner was born.

Nora shook off the memory. "A manacle! It's held captive by a . . ."

Rip stepped out of the corn. "Robbie!" he roared.

The Provisioner spun around and the two brothers stood face to face for the first time in twelve years.

Chapter Twenty-three

Anil Avatar had not slept for two days. Officer Monday called him every morning at nine o'clock to give him an update, though the news was always the same: Satchel Nolan was still being held in the Waitsfield jail; another child had woken up with the zombie sickness; Nora Sweetkale was still missing.

What Avatar knew was that there would be no update, no real news to report, unless he accepted the fact that things had happened—and were still happening—that could not be explained. Until he was ready to do that, nothing would change.

So he had been doing jigsaw puzzles. He did them out in his garden, the puzzle spread out on a folding table. It was an activity that relaxed him and allowed his mind to wander far away and then come hurtling back. After two days of this, he was ready to talk to Meg Nolan and tell her what he knew.

It was barely light out when he stood on the doorstep of the Nolan house, preparing to ring the bell. It turned out he didn't have to. The door simply opened, and a weary-looking Meg appeared.

"The coffee's on," she said, waving him in.

They had not become friends in the past weeks—Avatar would not go that far—but an undeniable respect for each other had developed. He followed Meg into the kitchen.

"Twelve years ago something happened," he blurted out to her pink-robed back.

Meg said nothing. She rummaged around in the cabinets for mugs.

"Something I could never explain," he continued. "Something so strange, so abnormal I tried to forget it . . ."

Meg poured coffee into the mugs. She sat down slowly, her lips pursed into a thin line. She did not know exactly what Avatar was about to say, but she knew the conversation had been brewing since the day they had met. She had been waiting for him to approach her, but now she felt afraid.

In the past few weeks Avatar had proven himself to be a man of his word. Satchel was still in custody, but Avatar made sure he was treated well, with respect, and she and Billy were allowed to visit him whenever they wanted. Avatar himself came to the house every few days with groceries, magazines and newspapers, and videos for Billy. He had done his best to minimize their sense of isolation. Not for one moment had he treated them like criminals. Still, one could never be sure.

". . . until Nora Sweetkale's disappearance. Until that day I came to talk to you and Billy"—Avatar looked down at the table— "and saw those markings on the palms of his hands."

He said this quietly, respectfully. He didn't want to bully Meg. He wanted to become her ally. One of the things he had figured out during those long days of jigsaw puzzles was that he and Meg were linked in some way through Nora Sweetkale. Each had a responsibility to the girl.

"I had seen those markings once before," he said. He looked Meg straight in the eyes. She held his gaze steadily. "On the day Nora Sweetkale was born."

Meg was visibly startled. She had expected him to say something about Billy, or about windows, for many times in Avatar's presence windows had inadvertently popped open; Billy was still not in complete control of his gift. Time after time Meg had watched Avatar witness the windows appearing, and she had seen him choose to say nothing. But Nora Sweetkale's birth? This she had not expected.

"I'm sorry," Avatar said. "Clearly you have no idea what I'm talking about. Will you let me explain?"

Meg nodded.

"I retired from the Waitsfield police force a while ago. I worked there for thirty-eight years. I was the police chief."

"I know." Meg had known from the first he wasn't some rookie detective.

"Of course you do," said Avatar. "I'll get to the point. Twelve years ago we got a call. A disturbance coming from an apartment in a tenement building. I was alone that day in the station. I knew the area, and I was the first on the scene. I busted open the door and found a dead woman on the bed and next to her a baby who was alive but badly in need of attention. It was not pretty."

Avatar grimaced, remembering the blood, the soiled bedding, the stench in the room.

"Sitting in a chair next to the bed was a man. I'll never forget him. The look in his eyes. I asked him, 'Why did you let this happen?' because it was clear he had witnessed the birth and hadn't gotten any help for the woman.

"He said nothing. I walked over to the kitchen table. There was a book there, a blue book with the imprint of an anchor on the cover. I picked it up and the man gasped, as though I had put a knife through him." Avatar frowned, remembering. "He sank to the floor, doubled over in pain. It was the strangest thing."

Meg said nothing. Obviously the man was a Gatemaker and Avatar had unwittingly picked up his Ancora.

" 'Put it down,' the man ordered, but I didn't, and he stood up and began moving toward me. I pulled my gun, but he didn't stop. I shot him in the legs. Twice. It should have crippled him, but this man was abnormally powerful. 'Give me the book!' he screamed, still moving toward me. 'I'll shoot you again, mister,' I told him, 'and not in the legs this time.'

"That seemed to stop him. He turned as if his strength was being leached out of him. Then he gave a roar. He swung his arms up quickly, flashing the palms of his hands at me, and I saw markings, like tattoos. Blue squares within squares. Exactly the same markings that are on Billy's hands."

Meg nodded, knowing she and Avatar had traveled too far together in the past weeks, too far in this conversation, for her to deny it any longer.

Avatar continued his story. "There was a crackling sound out in the hallway. Blue sparks flew from his palms. Before I could stop him, he staggered across the room and into the hallway and disappeared. You understand? He disappeared. He walked into the hallway and was gone."

Avatar reached out and clasped Meg's arm. "The air turned solid. It shrank. It peeled back."

Meg nodded again.

"You know what I'm talking about? It happens when Billy's around?"

"Yes, it does," said Meg, not quite ready to explain about Gatemakers, but willing to verify what he had seen.

Avatar exhaled loudly. He had been holding his breath without knowing it. Perhaps he had been waiting all his life for this moment; for somebody to confirm that there was more to the world than could be explained. More mystery. More wonder. More grace. He felt grateful to this fiery woman who sat in front of him. He knew it was not the moment to ask her to explain further.

"Shall I continue?" he asked.

"Please," she said softly.

"There was a pad of paper on the bedside table with the name *Nora* written on it. It was underlined twice."

Meg sighed. "Nora was told her parents died in an airplane crash when she was two weeks old."

"That was a lie. It happens all the time. When these cases get handed over to the adoption bureau, someone makes a decision about revealing the true circumstances of the baby's birth. In this case, those in charge decided it would have lessened her chances of getting adopted."

Meg shook her head angrily. "It would not have lessened Pauline Sweetkale's desire to adopt her. Somebody was wrong about that, and somebody was wrong in thinking Nora wouldn't want this information someday."

"I understand that," said Avatar. "On the day of my retirement, the blue book was brought to me and I sent it to her." He flushed, still ashamed at the police department's oversight.

"But why in the world would you send it now?" asked Meg, realizing that Avatar had unwittingly put everything in motion.

"Guilt. Fear. And shame," said Avatar. "The book belonged to Nora, and somebody had left it in a basement to rot."

"Why were you afraid?" asked Meg.

"Did you touch the book? Did you hold it?" Avatar asked.

Meg shuddered at that thought of Avatar holding an Ancora that didn't belong to him, but she was even more disturbed by the fact that Nora had bonded with her father's Ancora.

"It's called an Ancora," explained Meg. "And no, I didn't touch it. I would know better than to do that. It's a huge breach of etiquette. Actually, that's an understatement. By picking up that man's Ancora you began to kill him."

Avatar stared at Meg. Never had he heard such things. Never would he have believed them until now.

"Well, it made me sick when I touched it. The book felt alive— like it had a life of its own," he remembered. "I figured it was Nora's only legacy. She should have it. I had no idea it would cause so much trouble."

They sat in silence for a while, then Meg exhaled loudly. "Things might have happened this way without Nora having the Ancora. You can't be sure it was responsible for all of this."

"I can't," he said. "But I'm sure it's related."

"It is related," Meg agreed. "Her having it probably made a bad situation even worse."

Avatar's face sagged.

"So what do you want?" Meg asked finally. "You have some idea of what we are, who we are, that we're not normal. What do you want from us?"

"I want to help you," said Avatar firmly.

"But why would you want to help us? You know we're involved in some way, and that things are not as they appear."

"Why wouldn't I?" asked Avatar, rising from the table. "I walked into that girl's life just hours after she was born. The question you should be asking me, that you should all be asking me, is where the hell have I been?"

Chapter Twenty-four

Billy was astonished. Not that Rip was standing in front of him, although this *was* surprising; he had given up on finding him nights ago. What was astonishing was the resemblance that still existed between the Provisioner and Rip. Billy blinked, trying to make sense of what he was seeing. Even though the Provisioner's face was like a hide, thickened and metallic-looking, the two men had identical features.

Rip, too, was fighting a flood of emotions. He was overjoyed at finding his brother, but bewildered as well. Who had done this to him and why? But mostly he wondered what terrible harm his brother had done and how many children were dead because of him.

And then Rip made a decision: He would stop his brother. Filled with terrible love and unbearable sadness for them all, Rip leapt forward to begin a battle that would not end until one or both of them were dead. At the same moment the Provisioner leapt forward, too, bellowing a war cry.

The brothers met, crashing into each other so hard the ground shook. They began to wrestle, each trying to hammer the other down. The air was filled with the sound of their grunts. Rip was forced to the ground first, and the Provisioner towered above him, grinding his face into the dirt with its foot.

"The manacle!" Nora cried out.

Rip reached under the furs, his hands grappling the Provisioner's ankles. He found the circlet of metal on its right leg. Desperately Rip searched for a clasp, some way to get the manacle off. There was none. He tried to ram the manacle down the Provisioner's leg. That didn't work, either. It seemed to get even tighter, as if it knew it was in danger of being dislodged.

The Provisioner knelt down and picked Rip up. With a mighty roar it lifted him over its head and threw him across the clearing. Rip fell hard but tumbled smoothly and rolled up into a crouch.

"You've got to get it off!" shouted Billy. "It's the only way."

Rip nodded grimly. From his pocket he drew out a small but sharp knife. The blade shimmered.

"Are you going to try and cut it off?" Nora was confused. The manacle was enchanted; a knife would be worthless.

Rip shook his head. "Cut *him* off it."

"You mean cut its leg off?" asked Billy. "You would do that?"

Rip nodded. "Do you see another way? He's got to be stopped."

Nora looked frantically from one to the other. She knew this wouldn't solve anything. "Let me go back in. Send me back to the last memory. Billy, I want to go inside my father."

Billy shuddered. One glimpse of Nora's father had made it clear he was a treacherous, evil man. Billy hesitated.

"He said the manacle has been in his family for years. He must know!" Nora insisted.

"Do it," said Rip, bracing himself as the Provisioner hurled down upon him again.

Back they went into the memory of the library.

Nora's father sighed. "Take it, my friend. It will make your life better. I promise you."

Robbie looked at the metal braid again. "What does it do?"

At this exact moment Billy began the process of entering Armadon's mind. Like a long-distance runner, he knew he would have to pace himself. It was a delicate process that he was undertaking, and he was pushing the limits of his power.

He tried to visualize what he was doing. He had opened the doorway to the Provisioner's memory and closed it behind him. Now he was standing in a dark passageway. It took a while for his eyes to adjust to the lack of light, and then he saw it, way down at the other end of the corridor—another door. This was the doorway he had to open. The doorway inside of the door. It was like one of those painted wooden dolls. You opened the doll up, and inside was another doll, only smaller.

Painstakingly, Billy began to walk down that passageway. It was like trying to rip steel with his teeth. The air got thinner as he walked forward, for he was doing something unnatural, forcing the membrane of the Provisioner's memory apart. The last few steps were torturous. His body felt split in two, his lungs close to bursting. Finally, he stood at the doorway.

"I'm here," he gasped. "You sure you want to do this?"

"Yes," said Nora calmly.

With one quaking hand Billy reached down and opened the door.

Amusement. Pleasure. Robbie's hand scrabbling about desperately trying to get the manacle off.

The giant of a man looked up at Armadon in bewilderment with the eyes of a betrayed child. For a moment Armadon was taken aback. Something pierced through him, some dim memory of a baby's cry, but he buried it deeply and went back to watching with the detached and analytical eye of a scientist.

Robbie's hands still clutched at the manacle, even after his skin had turned to hide and his irises had yellowed and he had transformed into a monster that would now prey on children. Like a snake with its head severed he was still searching for a return to life. Armadon chuckled. It would never be rid of the manacle, for it would come off only if someone told this loathsome creature "I love you." Armadon clapped his hands together, delighted with the beauty of it, the purity. The most potent artifacts were enchanted in the same twisted way. For who would say "I love you" to such a being as the Provisioner?

Nora scuttled out of her father's mind and fell onto the library floor, panting with exertion. Then she climbed out of the Provisioner's head and dropped onto the dirt of the cornfield.

"Did you find it?" Billy panted.

Nora nodded. She hoped she wasn't too late.

The two brothers had entered into a silent phase of their combat. They did not look each other in the eyes. Each looked only at the ground, head swinging like a pendulum from left to right, collecting himself. There was a giant gash on Rip's forehead, and his hair was dark with blood. His knife was now in the Provisioner's hand.

Shakily, Nora stood up. Without the anesthetic properties of the Kapth, her arm throbbed horribly. She cradled it against her chest and struggled to fend off a rising sense of vertigo. "Rip! You must tell him what he most wants to hear. What nobody else will tell him!"

The incantation would not work unless the words were uttered freely. This was the nature of the enchantment. Nora could not tell Rip what words to say.

Rip was watching the blade of his knife glinting in the Provisioner's hand. Slowly the knife began to descend toward him. "I don't know what to do!" he cried.

"You do. Remember who he used to be!" yelled Nora.

Rip squeezed his eyes shut, not wanting this monster's face to be the last thing he saw before he died. He wanted to see Robbie's face, and so he called it up, the gentle man who had always been under his protection, his twin brother who meant more to him than anything in the world.

"Robbie boy, I love you," he said, a second before the knife buried itself in his flesh.

The manacle fell from the Provisioner's leg and darted frantically about on the ground as if in search of something.

"Get it!" shouted Nora. But neither she nor Billy moved. They were too exhausted, each in a world of private pain. It wouldn't have mattered if they had anyway, for the manacle was preternaturally fast and it slithered away through the corn. They followed the brilliant blue flickering with their eyes.

Freed of the thing that had held it captive, the Provisioner swayed from side to side and began to keen. Its mouth opened in a wide O, its lips stretched taut against its teeth. The thickened metallic hide began to soften like wax. Wrinkles materialized, deep tributaries on either side of its mouth. Rivers of ruddy-colored human skin ran down its limbs, streamed up its neck and across its broad face, and a man began to emerge as if from a cocoon, his eyes furiously blinking. When the transformation was complete, he pitched forward onto the ground.

Rip groaned and struggled to sit up. A steady stream of blood seeped out from his belly, but the wound wasn't deep; the blade hadn't penetrated the vital organs.

"The souls," Billy cried out. "He's got to relinquish the souls!"

Rip flinched and looked down at his brother. He knew what had to be done. He would have to cram the bit into his brother's mouth, forcing him to retch up all the souls he had stolen, all the lives that were not his. He also knew this would kill his brother, for Robbie's soul had been stolen long ago, and without the surrogate souls he would not survive.

Robbie began to moan, tossing his head from side to side.

"You must put the bit in his mouth." Billy tossed the bridle to Rip.

The big man obeyed, although clearly it hurt him to do so. He stuffed the bit into his brother's mouth, and Robbie began to gag. He convulsed and writhed as Rip patiently held him down. The stolen souls came out of his mouth one at a time. They were translucent ribbons, each nearly twenty feet long, and as soon as they hit the air they corkscrewed and made sorrowful noises.

"What do we do with them?" asked Rip.

"We do nothing," said Billy. "They'll find their way home."

Sure enough, the souls floated away in search of their children.

When it was done, when his brother was emptied, Rip stood up slowly, exhaling heavily. He threw the bridle to the ground in disgust. "You'll need to get rid of that bit."

"I know," said Billy. He could see the bit was made from the same indigo metal as the manacle.

Rip pressed his hand hard against his belly for a moment, trying to stanch the flow of blood. His brother lay on the ground, broken, near death now. Rip forgot about his wound and bent down to pick Robbie up gently. It was an amazing sight, one Billy would never forget.

Nora hadn't spoken for a while. Now that the crisis was over, she was finding the pain of her broken arm overwhelming. She thought she might pass out.

"She's bad off," said Rip. "You'll need to come up with a story." His mouth worked furiously, as if he were chewing on something. "Alma," he said finally. "The old woman at the fairgrounds. She'll cover for you. Your father has always been good to us. He brings us blankets in the winter and gives us vegetables and jugs of cider. Tell her who you are. She'll help you out."

Then Rip walked quickly into the corn, cradling his brother in his arms. When he was out of sight they heard him call out once more. "I believe in everything. Risk. Doorways. Forgiveness . . ." His voice drifted off. The night swallowed him up, and he was gone.

*　　*　　*

Twenty minutes later, Pauline Sweetkale got a call from Waitsfield Hospital. David had woken up.

237

Chapter Twenty-five

*E*ven though the doorway between Sanasarea and Waitsfield had been sealed up, Asa waited, just in case Nora and Billy needed his help. After an hour had passed, he knew his waiting was pointless. They would not call on him. They *could* not call on him. Whatever was happening in Waitsfield was Nora and Billy's responsibility. It was their destiny, not his.

Feeling utterly useless, he walked through the corn back down to his boat. He was swamped with loneliness. He wasn't sure he was capable of keeping the promise he had made to Nora; he wanted nothing more than to go back to Trout Island, lock himself in the lilac cottage, and never come out. The undertow of his old reclusive life was insistent.

When he reached the rowboat, the ruby-colored doublecat was waiting for him. She lay sprawled over the gunwales, dozing lazily in the last of the day's sun. When she saw Asa, she yawned and rolled over on her back, paws up in the air, exposing her stomach.

Asa cried out with happiness, not realizing until now how very much he had missed her. A sense of purpose flowed through him once more. He reached into the boat to rub Tria's stomach. She purred wildly, her giant head butting his arm.

"Where have you been, girl?" Asa whispered. He didn't know that Tria had gone far, far away; that she had loved a boy. But it didn't matter, for Asa belonged to Tria and she belonged to him, no matter how far each had traveled. Asa stroked the doublecat's silky coat and buried his face in her sweet fur.

✳   ✳   ✳

Molly had decided that the information about the Map could wait, but Roane could not. As exciting as it was to finally succeed in the Deeps, it paled beside her concern for her brother. Unknowingly Molly Berry had unearthed the greatest artifact of all: her heart.

When she walked into Roane's room, the boy was sitting facing the window. This was the way he spent all his days. Molly dragged a chair up beside him. She had spent countless hours with Roane looking out at the Greenwater Sea. She had grown to savor the silence, drawing comfort from the knowledge that they were both looking at the same thing. Nothing, *nothing* mattered more than this.

"See anything, Mol?"

Her brother's voice floated out of the silence.

Stunned, Molly turned to Roane. He smiled at her shyly, as if meeting her for the first time.

She nodded. "You," she whispered, "I see you."

Chapter Twenty-six

Billy staggered up the deck steps with Nora on his back. She was moaning softly. The kitchen door of the Nolan house flew open, and Meg ran out, Avatar at her heels.

"Nora!" Meg cried.

"Don't touch her," panted Billy. "She's hurt."

Avatar looked Nora over quickly, noting her labored breathing, the way her left arm dangled limply at her side. He leaned in close so that he could see her face. She looked feverish, eyes glazed, cheeks flushed, but she appeared to be okay.

"Nora, my name is Avatar," he said quietly. "You'll need to slide off Billy's back yourself. I don't want to touch you. I'm pretty sure your arm is broken. Can you do that?"

She looked at him dully. "Who are you?" she croaked. He looked familiar, but she couldn't place him.

"He's a friend," said Meg. "You can trust him. He's here to help."

Nora nodded. Billy lowered her gently to the ground until her feet touched the deck.

"Over here," said Meg, leading her to a chaise. Nora lay down carefully, holding her injured arm tight to her chest.

"You need to see a doctor," said Avatar.

"Not yet," said Nora.

Meg was watching Avatar carefully. She was impressed by the way he dealt with Nora, who looked horrible. Her clothes were torn and stained, and she smelled foul, a mixture of vomit and sweat, yet Avatar didn't flinch. He was gentle, but he didn't baby her.

Billy was slumped in a chair, still trying to catch his breath from the long walk carrying Nora through the fields. His hands were filthy from digging a deep hole to bury the bit. Meg wanted to gather him up in her arms but thought better of it. She didn't know exactly what had happened, but it was clearly tremendous. Billy had crossed the threshold from boy to young man, from outcast to Gatemaker.

"What happened?" she asked him.

"She came back," Billy said, eyeing Avatar warily.

"Through your doorway?" the retired chief asked.

"You told him?" Billy cried.

Meg shook her head. "I didn't tell him anything. I didn't have to. He knew. He's known all along."

Nora gave a soft little moan from the chaise.

"Oh, lamb," said Meg, and ran to her side. She stroked Nora's cheek tenderly. "What can I get for you?"

"The Ancora," whimpered Nora. "In my knapsack."

The knapsack was on the steps where Billy had dropped it. Avatar brought it over. Meg knew better than to touch the Ancora. She undid the clasp and opened the mouth of the knapsack wide, allowing Nora to pull the blue book out herself. Trembling, Nora laid it on her chest. The others watched in amazement as the Ancora quivered and for a split second transformed into its bird form, nestling into Nora's clothes, its breast heaving, feathers twitching. A second later it was a book once more.

Billy was shocked. Because of his telepathy he had always known about Nora's blue book, but now that he actually saw it he found himself overwhelmed with grief.

"What is it?" he gasped.

Meg realized she had forgotten to tell Billy about Ancoras. He had no way of making sense of the sadness that was now enveloping him, for he was past the age when his Ancora should have been presented to him. Instead his Traveler had an Ancora, and Billy had nothing.

"Don't be afraid," said Meg. "You have one, too." And it was true, Billy did. Somewhere at the Aquisto was his Ancora, waiting for him.

"Well, where is it?" Billy asked.

"It's in Talfassa," she said with resignation, knowing that someday both Billy and Nora would have to go back to Greenwater. But Meg could not bear to think of that yet. Her answer seemed to satisfy Billy for now, since he realized there were more pressing matters to attend to: Nora's condition, for one.

Once Nora had the Ancora, her breathing quieted. It was not unpleasant for her anymore, being bound to it. She knew now that she could never be separated from it. It contained the unsavory story of her father's life, but within his story was her own. She would not turn away.

Accepting this fact put her strangely at ease. There were two sides of her life that were very different from each other, but there was room enough for both. Now she chose to be Nora Sweetkale: seventh-grader, best friend of Billy Nolan, lover of thin-crust pizza and Scrabble.

"I miss my mother," Nora said forlornly.

Avatar was not sure which mother she was referring to. "There are things you should have been told," he said. "Things that should not have been kept from you."

Billy interrupted. "The Provisioner's dead."

It was Meg's turn to gasp. "But how?"

Billy shook his head, not wanting to relive the encounter, not yet. "Call the hospital," he said with authority.

Avatar looked at him questioningly but went. He disappeared into the house to make the call. When he came back he was shaking his head in disbelief. "I could hear the children laughing in the background. It's as if they were never sick."

Billy nodded. "Now call the police station. Tell them Nora Sweetkale's returned. Release my father," he commanded.

"They'll want to know where she's been," said Avatar.

Billy eyed him coolly. He felt the same way he had when he had first communicated with Nora telepathically, deeply grounded in himself, in his powers. He gave Avatar the story.

"The night Nora disappeared, she, too, was stricken with the zombie sickness, only she was older, so she didn't get it as bad as the younger children; she only lost her memories. She's been living at the fairgrounds. She didn't know where home was; she didn't even know she *had* a home; that's why she's been missing all this time. Your people can check that with an old woman named Alma who lives at the fairgrounds. She's been looking after Nora."

Avatar was impressed. It was a good story. And if this Alma

was willing to corroborate it, pretty much airtight. He knew the fairgrounds were a refuge for the homeless. Over the years he had instructed his staff to leave them alone. The people who lived there were harmless, and he had been glad they'd managed to fashion shelters for themselves out of the abandoned concession stands.

"The broken arm?" Avatar asked, wanting to make sure they covered everything.

"She fell off the old Ferris wheel," Billy said, remembering the rusted-out rides. "She hit her head as well, and that's how her memories returned."

"Right," said Avatar, wondering just who was in charge.

Nora turned her face to the side, searching for Billy's eyes. "Come here," she whispered.

Billy walked over to the chaise and knelt down. Nora wrapped her good arm around his neck and drew him close.

"It's time for me to go home. Will you take me home now, Billy?"

And so he did.